High Hopes

High Hopes

Quest of a Queer, Neurodivergent, Stoner Scientist

Miyabe Shields, PhD

To the legacy cannabis community who saved me,

To the neurodivergent cannabis community who sees me,

And to everyone who has supported me.

"Our indigenous herbalists say to pay attention when plants come to you; they're bringing you something you need to learn."

Dr. Robin Wall Kimmerer, PhD

- - - - - - -

"I see the job of the scientist, in part, as helping to correct the blunders of politicians and journalists."

Dr. Carl Hart, PhD

- - - - - - -

"Has not society itself helped to make the individual unhealthy? Of course, the unhealthy must be made healthy, that goes without saying; but why should the individual adjust himself to an unhealthy society? [...] Without first questioning the health of society, what is the good of helping misfits to conform to society?"

Jiddu Krishnamurti

This quote is sometimes interpreted as:

"It is no measure of health to be well-adjusted to a profoundly sick society."

Table of Contents

Supplemental Information:

"Isn't it funny how danger makes people passionate?"

Zelda Fitzgerald

(Obligatory) Author Disclosure

Please note this book is listed as fiction - all human memory is surprisingly unreliable (which really makes you think a lot about the fragility of reality, am I right?). But first and foremost this is a story with many details shifted, emphasized, or completely removed, and everything given from the perspective of a self-admittedly "unreliable narrator."

At one point it actually said so on my medical records, so while I considered writing in a magical dragon to fly me away from reality, I chose to state universally and without any doubts: this book is fiction.

All content in this book, including text and images, are not meant to be medical advice and do not substitute for, or supplement medical or professional advice given by a medical provider or otherwise. For any and all medical issues, including lifestyle and health issues, the reader is advised to consult their personal physician and to abide by their recommendation. The author acknowledges that science is ever-evolving and the cannabis and cannabinoid space is an especially accelerated research topic. All scientific information included was written in a good faith effort to make an accurate representation of the data findings at the time of publication.

"I gave my life to become the person I am now. Was it worth it?"

Richard Bach

Introduction by Laine Shields

I was 16 when I started having severe, near-daily migraine attacks, the pain too searing to consider leaving bed. My brain was a constant state of depression and anxiety. Desperate for a cure, I visited a merry-go-round of doctors who prescribed a list of pharmaceuticals including painkillers, sedatives, anxiolytics, and antidepressants. My teenage years were a haze of chronic fatigue and brain fog, as the medicine dulled my senses and my migraine disorder intensified.

At 17 I was diagnosed with a brain tumor; I was ecstatic when the surgeon told me that I would wake up pain free, and that I would be able to walk out of the hospital that same day.

But when we drove to New York City for surgery, the surgeon removed a part of my healthy pituitary gland — in fact, the tumor diagnosis was a mistake. I awoke in unbearable pain and was unable to walk on my own for 3 weeks. My migraines persisted and my pill intake snowballed, now forced to compensate for my lack in hormone production.

During my recovery, I was rushed back to the hospital with a massive brain bleed. I heard the emergency responders panicking around me, shouting, "I don't think we'll make it unless we take a helicopter."

I nearly died that day, and I used to wish that I had.

When I was 21, I attempted suicide with the same pharmaceuticals that were supposed to save me. I awoke from a week-long coma, burnt out on conventional medicine and determined to find another path.

For me, it turned out that path was a person.

I met Miyabe when I was 23 and spending 5 days per week in some part of an active migraine attack cycle, still on heavy pharmaceuticals. Miyabe had just experienced their own near-death experience (*Chapter 4*) and if we hadn't met, I'm not sure either one of us would have made it.

Miyabe was a breath of fresh air, a reprieve from the darkness. For the first time in my life, I could envision an actual future. We meshed in endless ways, but I particularly treasured our shared fascination with the brain, behavior, and drugs.

By the time we met, I had turned my passion into a career teaching neurodivergent students how to adapt to a neurotypical world. While I helped equip others, I was simultaneously struggling to understand my own brain and why western medicine had repeatedly failed me.

My migraine journey was long and winding, but Miyabe's scientific approach to self-experimentation with cannabis sparked something in me that eventually helped me find an exit from dependence on pharmaceuticals.

Mind-altering drugs can teach us a lot about our brains.

They offer a fresh perspective, enabling a deeper exploration of our own cognitive processes. They show us an overwhelming truth: we all experience the world around us in a profoundly unique way.

This means we all have diverse experiences with drugs, for better or for worse. Drugs can give us relief. Or they can give us pain. At their core they alter us, and that is the point. That's one reason why I love exploring what another person's favorite drug is. It tells you a lot about them.

You can probably guess already that Miyabe's is cannabis. But if you asked me? Miyabe is my favorite drug. And you're about to find out why.

Laine Shields, M.Ed
Accessible Education Specialist
@transitionabilities

1. It All Started in AP Bio...

"You've really never smoked weed?" My TA's ice-blue eyes were piercing through the top of my head and boring their way through my thoughts like an industrial drill press, "your brain would be interesting on drugs."

Would it?

The truth was I had, technically, kind of, sort of already smoked weed... or at least I thought so...

The problem was that I couldn't really remember.

My gateway experience was definitely alcohol: the year prior I downed a vile concoction that was 50/50 Sauza and orange Gatorade. This was followed by several shots of SoCo. I was later told the rest of that night involved forties, cigarettes, and hookah. Then at some point I took a single hit off a joint before immediately vomiting in the bushes and passing out on the brick and stucco ledge where I awoke in the early morning hours covered in bug bites in places where absolutely no one should ever have bug bites (which, unfortunately, was an experience I ended up repeating twice more).

I was fourteen years old at the time and that was just the first taste of my reckless approach to drugs, the long feast to follow.

The hangover and overall grossness of the whole experience deterred me from alcohol for about half a year, but I quickly found my way back after that, and with a vengeance. Cigarettes were the natural encore act.

As with so many others who were raised with the D.A.R.E. approach that preached total abstinence from all drug use with no practical safety or science information, the clear omission of information only heightened my desire to seek drug experiences out. The mantra I remember well is that "only losers do drugs." But I didn't care about becoming a "loser," because I already was a "loser." For my entire youth up until I found cannabis, I was as uncool as they come.

I was socially atypical, selectively mute, and overweight. I wore transition sunglasses (still do) and was taunted as "Snorlax" on the playground. I lacked total understanding of what I should or shouldn't do or say to make it stop.

I lacked total understanding of how to interact with others in general.

I also grow a strong mustache for someone female at birth and so pictures of me in yearbooks or on the wall would all eventually end up with extra inked mustaches and unibrows added on. If I was already uncool, what did I have to lose?

On top of all that, my D.A.R.E. officers all looked like "losers" to me, so that angle was doubly ineffective.

But by far the biggest driving force of my early experimentation was the momentary relief of not being trapped in my own mind. My brain was my every day, every hour living hell for as long as I could remember. Since the beginning of my memory I have been in some combination of physical, mental, and/or emotional pain.

It definitely sucked the most when it felt completely out of control.

So altering my mind state to be anything different, even if it wasn't necessarily better, was still a net positive and still an unbelievably strong draw.

By the time I was in high school, I had been hiding self-injurious behaviors for years, which was especially challenging as a swimmer and water polo player. I remember one of my teammate's mom's remarking to me, "you should never do that to yourself," and thinking back silently, "but it's the only thing that makes my brain stop."

And if my brain kept going it would eventually end up at suicide. One of my earliest memories is lying with my face pressed into the coarse, curly tan carpet wishing I had never been born and hoping that some accident would just take me without me having to actually do anything. That's not to say I didn't have joy in my childhood, but just that the joy was like flashing bright sparks in an extreme contrast of darkness.

The powerful sedation of alcohol was blissful and it served as the entry point into searching for other potentially useful modifications to my brain.

It was around the same time that I started experimenting with drugs that I found out that all humans weren't suicidal as a default state of being, which surprised me. Up until then, I just assumed everyone felt the same way I did and was just better at hiding it. Until then I thought everyone was experiencing what I was.

"I could make it happen, you know," my TA continued, finally looking away to the animal physiology paintings on the walls, withdrawing his icicle spears and allowing me to start to conceptualize the proper response. "I could drop you off at home so you wouldn't have to drive."

I looked at his careless blonde curls and my chest pressurized with longing. I wanted to be closer, to connect more deeply. It was an all-too-familiar feeling.

Every time I got kind of close with someone, I would find myself faced with one unexpected detour to another detour to another detour, always circling the destination, but never quite getting there. I couldn't help but watch the way others progressed to form a bond that I seemed to be unable to achieve.

It was an insurmountable barrier that I couldn't even fully conceptualize; I just always remained a little bit on the outside. I moved schools a lot up until my second high school, so I became versed in meeting new people. But this feeling always cropped up when I wanted to become more than just the new kid in town. It was like trying to get any sort of firm grip on something impossibly slippery that was always changing to water as my hands failed to take hold.

The feeling wasn't romantic, or at least I don't think it was... (I still struggle with identifying different emotional states and depths of relationships) I think it was just an overwhelming desire to be "real friends" and not the multi-layered facade I had adopted, not the complex code of scripting I analyzed and performed to be able to navigate the California public school system. I could see how other humans simply were with each other and I could feel how I was simply not on the same page, especially in person.

But this TA and I had been chatting over AIM (AOL Instant Messenger, an early internet chat messaging application), and that felt more real than anything I had ever experienced before. Our chats always began about a boring shared event from school and ended with us questioning reality or questioning ways to prove reality's existence.

He was also a local plug, or source, for a number of things, but mainly cannabis and psychedelics. He regularly came to school high as a kite, eyes blood-red, demolishing two donuts in English and laughing through our socratic seminars. It did look like fun. And he was always fine by lunch time.

"Yeah, okay."

His eyes speared directly back into mine, their unexpected force on the back of my skull zapped my eyes down to my desk. "Whaaaaaaaaaat?!" I could tell by his voice he wore a cheshire grin and my heartbeat doubled in speed, pounding against my ribs, "I'll wait for you by your locker after school. And I'll get the whole crew together!"

A few hours later I was sitting out of sight in the bushes on the side of a casual slope with the "Hillcrest Crew" assembled around me. As my luck would have it, they had just picked up a brand new glass bong and "a quarter" to break it in. It was about eight inches tall made of orange and yellow opaque colored glass that swirled around a circular base up the stem.

"Got the chronic," someone said before producing a gallon-sized ziplock bag half full with puffy dried plant material. A quarter is slang for one quarter of one pound and since one pound is 453 grams, a quarter is around 114 grams (or it should be, since in my experience all the greatest sources are generous and round up) of the flowering portion of the cannabis plant which contains the active molecules. It was quite a bit of flower.

I would learn later on that my first time was pretty extraordinary.

People say you don't get high the first time. And I've got some theories as to why (I think it has to do with membrane saturation, an extensive depot effect, and differential receptor signaling in naive brains). Some brains may become more sensitive to recognizing more subtle effects after experience, but the undeniable effects can be overcome with enough dosage.

Well, I had the dosage.

I sat with the crew in a circle and each of them packed a snap (a small personal bowl for a single hit on a bong), smoked it down (called "milking the bong"), before handing it to me so I could pull out the bowl piece and "clear it." This went on for two full rotations before I hit an entire snap myself, milking the bong and clearing it, and we returned to a normal cycle, passing to the left.

A gentle veil wrapped around my brain and I felt everything shift slightly, like my head had expanded a bit and there was more space to move around with my thoughts.

I will never forget how soft and soothing the sound of the wind was as it gently brushed the branches against each other. It's not like I hadn't heard that exact sound before, but it was different. It was calming and reassuring. It was way less sharp.

Something I would learn later on was that I have what is called auditory hypersensitivity, which means my brain is extra sensitive to sounds. When a train or ambulance goes by, I have to imagine myself closing my ears off to stifle the pain. And I can always hear all the conversations happening around me, which other brains are capable of filtering out to better focus on only a few sounds at a time.

It sucks a lot of the time to be able to hear everything, but at other times it can have its advantages.

Auditory sensitivity is part of what enabled me to succeed academically, because most classes are built around listening to lectures and my brain has a good memory for sounds. Categorical thinking and rigidity to rules (which are both common traits for brains like mine) helped me, too, since science is basically founded upon sets of mathematical rules to boil down a snapshot of nature and then how true, living, breathing nature defies them, so then we search for more math to describe them and so on, and so on, and so on.

But those traits that I am told I have been "gifted" to receive also come with more burdensome atypicalities. My sensory sensitivities can still bring out an unexpected tantrum. Decreased sound sensitivity and increased auditory gating, the process of filtering out the excess noise, has been an important tool in the toolbelt. The first time I experienced it was memorable to say the least.

It was medicine from the start, I just didn't know it yet.

Getting high off my ass was the first time I felt like the world (and my existence) didn't have to be so painful. It made me feel like I could continue on, like I had something to strive towards. A mysterious wave of significance rang through my brain. "Maybe I could make my brain quieter like this all the time," I thought to myself, "Maybe I could even like being alive."

I remember the swish of those branches and when I looked up at their melodic dance, I smiled for real.

"So you like it." A clear voice from across the way asked. His voice was a new one. We had never talked before. I brought my gaze down, partly to see who it was but mostly because when people talk to you they expect you to look in their general direction or else it's considered rude.

I usually aim for the forehead, because it is close enough to be almost indiscernible from true eye contact for the other person, but sometimes I miss and at that exact moment my motor skills were pretty affected.

I missed the forehead. I was in the danger zone and I noticed he was looking back at me, too. It was going to happen, and my stomach lurched with dread. And then it did happen.

Our eyes **fully** met.

At first all I felt was disorienting confusion. It took a moment to process that I wasn't in pain. How unusual.

"You look surprised," he smiled and gave a small laugh before he was the one to look down, a little awkwardly.

I was more than surprised. I was experiencing something I never thought would happen. I was looking someone in the eyes while they were talking to me without any pain. His eyes were a stunning mix of gray, green, and light copper. I smiled back at him.

"Yeah, I **really** like it."

Everyone laughed and I felt something new stirring from deep within my core; it reached out and formed an invisible tie to everyone around me. I was sharing an experience and I was clicked into it with them; I was fully in it. Those gray eyes lit on me again and I laughed and laughed and laughed at the lack of pain.

I spent a lot of time looking into that first pair of eyes. He became a lot of my firsts - my first love, my first loss, and my first cannabis mentor.

On one of our early dates, we smoked in his car before walking along the cliffs in Laguna. I loved the feeling of the sand and filled my pockets with it so I could keep stimming, or repeating a movement that scratches an itch on the inside of my brain. I woke up the next morning, my jean shorts kicked to the end of the bed, with my sheets full of sand.

He never let me live that one down.

My first time would have been a fairy tale if I wasn't so prone to anxiety, but there's lessons to learn from the harshness of reality...

The onset of smoking is fast, usually full effects are felt in less than ten minutes, and so I felt it almost immediately when I crossed my limit that very first time. My thoughts became fragmented, disorganized, and a sharp edge had returned to all the sounds around me.

The change happened suddenly and it felt as if everything that was light and airy had turned dark and scary. My stomach curled itself up into a ball, which was a telltale sign of worse things to come. I didn't know what was happening, all I knew was that I was not. feeling. good.

I struggle to name emotions and rely upon a pretty complex analysis of the physical symptoms in my body and the greater context of the situation I'm in, a phenomenon called alexithymia. Anxiety for me is all stomach and clamminess. At a certain point I turn within myself and am forced to race around in my own brain in looping circular thought patterns that repeat over and over and over. It was getting difficult to speak and I became even more distressed.

The low rumble of a panic attack was gaining space around the bottom of my brain stem, a black, inky blotch spreading itself out and waiting for the right trigger to sever my control to my brain and body.

Luckily the Hillcrest Crew was an experienced bunch. They identified I had become anxious, pinpointed that I wanted to be by myself, assured me that it would definitely pass quickly, and drove me home where I immediately became paranoid about my dad smelling cannabis on me. In the state I was in, I rushed into what I thought the only solution could be... which was to shower... with all my clothes on.

In retrospect the damp clothes hanging in the bathroom were probably more suspicious than if I had just thrown them in the washer. The higher doses of cannabis can impair planning and critical thinking, especially in naive minds and/or combined with anxiety. But after the weirdly clothed shower and finding myself in a more familiar space at home, the paranoia and panic did pass. It took around an hour and a half, which is the average peak duration of a smoking dose before it begins to come down.

A few more hours later and all of the impairment had slipped away. My brain's main functionality returned to baseline, but the background humming was still lowered. I had found a new type of quietness from within that my brain lacked access to before. My thoughts felt like they were basking in a calm lake instead of being tossed around in the open ocean.

I woke up the next day feeling incredible, feeling undoubtedly changed, and feeling like I had finally found an option that didn't involve hurting myself.

There isn't just one single way that cannabis has helped me - it's an all-over net benefit. Most of the benefits I receive from cannabis can't even be felt until the day after or even longer after that. It would take me years and years to piece apart all the little separate effects, but it was immediately apparent from the very first experience how being high helped me relate to others.

Cannabis gave me the ability to explore social situations with a new perspective and helped me gain new abilities. Building experience with other young stoners while under the influence of cannabis helped me to go on to forge the relationships that saved me over and over again.

Community support of friends and family is the single most important factor in dictating the success of a person's recovery from trauma. I would not be here now if it weren't for a very large array of people who have been there to provide me with the right support at the right time.

I cannot stress enough how critical the role of cannabis was in my ability to create and maintain those relationships.

Things continued to improve from being able to meet someone's gaze and feel it gently to being able to build trusting, reciprocal relationships that have lasted through the very volatile periods of my young adulthood.

My first experience with firecrackers (basic DIY edibles created by mixing cannabis flower into peanut butter, smearing the mixture on top of crackers and microwaving it for short bursts of time to activate it, a process called decarboxylation or "decarbing") played a role in a Halloween theme park experience that was the beginning of my deepest lifelong friendship.

It felt like a superpower, like I had been given a pair of special glasses every time I was high that allowed me to understand what was going on in conversations and helped form how I should respond. I found my ability to find others. I found a connection my brain had been too overstimulated to see clearly before. And that connection changed everything for me. It is the first and most important way that cannabis contributed to my life.

After that first experience, I started heavily self-medicating with cannabis. I smoked everything I could get my hands on at every opportunity, which at the time was definitely much weaker than what's available now. But it did the trick. I smoked out of apples, empty soda cans, homemade gravity bongs, and eventually graduated to having my very own piece (slang for a smoking device, usually glass). I wanted to be high all the time. I loved feeling connected to other people and I loved feeling a quiet brain.

I am positive that at times it was too much. But I am also positive that the lasting effect it has had on my brain chemistry has been for the overall good. There has been a clear net benefit that I became more aware of once I learned how the system in the brain that interacts with cannabis controls social reward and overstimulation.

Of course, I have a strong bias. My bias comes from the lived experience of my brain with and without a fairly large number of substances. And the memory of what my brain was like before I was introduced to any of them.

I'm not going to sugarcoat it. I am definitely more neurodivergent than I appear and have displayed a lot of the more severe traits, meaning my brain functionality contains thoughts, processes, and behaviors outside the typical range. As a young child, I struggled with masking myself in school. I leaned towards aggression as an outlet - as anyone who played water polo against me would likely attest to. As a young adult I struggled with what was then diagnosed as many things including insomnia, depression, general anxiety, panic attack disorder, obsessive compulsive tendencies, mania, delusion, addiction, paranoia, and psychosis. Later it would be called a mis-diagnosis and would be renamed c-PTSD and autism, but I can no longer believe in labels when there's no biological basis.

But it is undeniable that I am part of the population that most medical professionals would say should never experiment with drugs due to differences in my executive functioning, emotional regulation, feelings of mysticism, and relatively loose understanding of reality. I find that ironic, because we are usually the population that experiments the most with drugs... because there is clearly a potential therapeutic application for us.

But I get why it's the safest recommendation to steer clear and always will be. Neurodivergent people can be predisposed to negative risks and side effects. I am definitely vulnerable to negative side effects, including anxiety, mood instability, dissociation, depersonalization, and developing dependencies.

The thing is... I have those same vulnerabilities to pharmaceuticals

It's hard to tell what was and wasn't brought on by the psychopharmaceuticals that I was put on without my full consent. And it's hard for me to value any categorization of mental health when there's pretty much no biological evidence for their separation.

The lack of validity of DSM diagnostic criteria has been a plague on our research and understanding of ourselves and our communities for decades. Diagnoses are socially constructed and it makes sense that a population who struggles with understanding social constructs would be the easiest to take advantage of and label the problem.

And honestly my most dangerous experiences with substances came from a rapid rotation of experimental cocktails of anti-anxiety, anti-depressant, sedative, and antipsychotic prescriptions in my late teens through early twenties. While they are absolutely valid, helpful medicines for some people, they destabilized me into someone beyond my own recognition. And it's never good not to recognize oneself.

It was my strong background experience with cannabis that coaxed the real me back into existence. Cannabis without a doubt saved me and it was a much closer call than I used to ever want to think about again.

But now I'm going to share it.

After losing the support of my medical professionals, stopping all my medications cold turkey (which I learned later is **very dangerous** and should never be done without supervision, ever), finding and paying for access to medical cannabis, and years of grueling, non-linear progress, my deeply internalized ableism, or prejudice and discrimination against disabilities, drove me to try to cure myself.

I thought getting my PhD in drug discovery in the system of the brain that interacts with cannabis, the endocannabinoid system, would solve my problematic brain by creating a pharmaceutical version of cannabis. I think part of me just simply wanted to understand, but the greater piece chose the pharmaceutical route with a desire to create a new, socially acceptable pill (or pills) to chomp down.

I was looking for something that could make me just a little bit more like everybody else. I wanted to change myself to fit in with society. But instead I found how to love and accept myself and now I want to change society.

I found that my experiences and the medical benefits I receive from cannabis are within the realm of reasonable scientific theory of neuropharmacology (the study of drugs in the brain), that I am not broken and that it's the system that needs fixing. There is ample scientific evidence that cannabis can be the best medicine for me (and others like me) and there is clear subjectivity in the interpretation of what the "net benefit" of any substance is for any specific individual.

Neurodiversity is a beautiful reality and we need to start embracing that reality in our approach to natural medicines as an equal alternative to pharmaceuticals. Especially natural medicines with an exponentially deeper medicinal history with humans than any synthetic compound. Especially with cannabis.

Because while cannabis is not for everyone (nothing is for everyone), some brains will benefit from a complex, naturally-occurring mixture of weaker molecules as opposed to a single, super strong pharmaceutical, or a cocktail of multiple pharmaceuticals. For some brains, this is the best medicine and learning how to optimize and harness it for its benefits can be a game changer.

We acknowledge that pain, sleep, and anxiety - the three most common uses of both medical and non-medical cannabis use - are all critical factors in regulating quality of life for those with complex mental health needs, but we shy away from taking the next logical step

Why are we so afraid to talk about it?

There is a compounding stigma when joining the topics of mental health and cannabis use, because there can be an increased vulnerability and there can be negative effects. But there can also be life-saving positive effects that have a relatively safe toxicity profile to the alternatives (other drugs, usually alcohol and pharmaceuticals). I have felt so alone in this exploration and it was enraging to find out that I am just one of far, far too many.

I hope to help build a safe space for this community to finally and fully come out of the closet and into the light.

2. Not of Sound Mind...

"So I am crazy?" My voice sounded separated, distant, and strangely metallic, like I was hearing myself speak through an old-school, spiral cord telephone.

"I didn't say that," my psychiatrist said in his gruff, mustache-y mumble, "I said you are confused"

Confused? Yes, I was confused. A couple months prior I had been sent to my university's health center by my water polo coaches for a dip in my athletic performance and had biked home less than two hours later with a prescription for zolpidem (Ambien). My brain had been patchy and disconnected ever since. It had lots of holes in it, giant gaping blank slots where my body had been present, but my brain had not.

I would wake up to my housemates laughing at my antics the night prior like slurring my way through a diatribe about how I once walked barefoot from California to Hawaii on a giant floating bridge. I was so adamant that I had partially convinced everyone before one of them actually had to look it up to refute me.

Another time I waltzed into the kitchen and announced I would make everyone hot chocolate. There were no takers, everyone politely declined, but I went on to rip open five packages at once and sprinkle them over a set of mugs on the kitchen counter. About half of the powder and dehydrated marshmallows made it to the relative vicinity of the mugs, and the rest I left on the counter. Then I splashed the cups half full with cold water from the sink, did not mix them, and forced them into my housemates' hands.

I have no memory of any of it.

It's clear to me now that I was having a negative reaction to the zolpidem (Ambien) and should have immediately ceased using it until I consulted with a professional. But I had made a grave, grave mistake that haunts me to this day. I didn't know what I was getting myself into; I couldn't fathom the intensity of altering one's mind with psychopharmaceuticals and the potential outcomes. I didn't understand what was happening. **I did not have proper informed consent**. And I didn't take the necessary precautions.

It was not on my radar at all that something like this could happen. When the nurse practitioner and pharmacist had given me all the warnings, I had been too flustered to really take it in. Plus even if I had understood the risks, I had no way of knowing what my next step would be. Even if I could identify a bad thing happening, I didn't know what to do next. I tend to need more direct guidance than most assume.

It would have benefited me to have a social narrative - or a sheet that outlines in third person what I would do in new or stressful situations. I was already having a difficult time and could barely handle organizing my day around filling that first prescription. On top of that I was too ashamed to trust another person with the full extent of my ignorance and what I viewed at the time as my personal deficit. I was alone in evaluating how these drugs were or weren't working for me, I was not a good judge of my own progress, and it cost me dearly.

In the weeks following the initial prescription, I had met with several therapists, a psychologist, and a psychiatrist. For clarification, these are the main three

Western, modern medical approaches to mental health, and they are all different.

Therapists connect emotionally and often use conversation, art, or other specific techniques to aid in navigating through difficult periods by processing memories and creating more self-awareness. It's not surprising that I would struggle to find support in a model that relies upon building a trusting relationship. I've been called "withdrawn" and "reluctant" and cannot count how many different types of therapists have said no to taking me on as a client. Usually the reason is because I would be a "high risk" or "high needs" client and they do not have the bandwidth for my caseload at that moment. It's not the sort of thing one likes to hear when the end of the rope is feeling slippery, but everyone's boundaries are important.

Psychologists are trained like scientists and receive a doctorate in psychology (PsyD) that is based in clinical (hospital-style) work and usually some form of research thesis. I've found their approach to be more scientific and I have had one great relationship with a psychologist who very openly embraced cannabis for neurodivergent adults. But he was my third of four psychologists I've tried to work with, and back during this first time around the psychologist clearly said that I most definitely, absolutely needed immediate help with medication and needed a psychiatrist.

So I had settled on this mustached psychiatrist and his cairn terrier, because he was a trained medical doctor (MD) whose purpose was to prescribe medicine, because he was the only one to take me on as a client, and because my brain wasn't so full of holes as to not recognize that I was in crisis.

The time it had taken me to find him and set up an appointment had been a rapid decline. I had started visibly losing weight and was pulling my hair out of the back of my head by my cowlick.

His first order of business had been to cut the zolpidem (Ambien) prescription in half. He said it had been too high for me, because it was based on my weight and I was heavy for my size. I've always been dense and have not been in the "normal" weight range for my height since I was seven. The weigh-ins for PE class played a part in earning me my "Snorlax" nickname. I remember hating the restaurant Claim Jumper, because they charge more for heavy kids and force kids to step up on a giant scale in the entryway before scribbling down the price on the paper menu. Humiliating.

My step dad would look down at me in disgust and make a comment about paying for an adult meal and keeping the leftovers. But everything in life has its pros and cons, and putting weight on altered his other behaviors towards me, so the body shaming was actually a net positive.

This psychiatrist also gave me alprazolam (Xanax) and what a truly wonderful experience that was, every time. Too wonderful, it turns out. But I wouldn't bear those consequences until much later. In the beginning, it was just an effective medicine, perhaps even a life-saving one, too. I felt like I was on the edge of panic all the time, like there was a knife pressed to my chest at the edge of cutting in. "Xannies" turned the knife to its broad side. The blade was still right there, but it was temporarily not a threat.

Once the panic attacks had quelled and I appeared to be sleeping more regularly, he told me that I "developed depression." That seemed funny to me, because it hardly seemed like a development - it was just my baseline. To me this deep and central darkness was always there, just under the surface, the space I was most familiar with withdrawing into. This was just the first time I was seeing someone whose job it was to medicate me for it.

But he said that was another thing that pills could fix and so I started taking fluoxetine (Prozac). We were a few weeks in and I didn't think things had changed substantially. Everything did seem a bit flatter. But my day-to-day volatility, holey-brain lack of memories, overall pharmaceutically-altered mindstate, water polo practices, and midterm exams made it difficult to self-report the summarized experience of an entire week in less than fifty minutes.

"You are confused, because a lot of things are changing." He continued in his slow and certain way.

Hot tears welled up and I held them back, blurring the bottom half of my vision as my nose began to stuff up. A sob creeped up my throat, but I clamped it down. I hated when people watched me cry, and I had been doing way too much of it in public in the past few months. And every time the psychiatrist saw me cry he would shake his head a bit and jot it down in his notebook. But the searing pain in my chest couldn't be stifled; instead, it flared brighter. A tiny, minuscule part of me was rebelling.

How could I be confused about this? If anything, it felt like the only thing I wasn't confused about. It felt like the only thing that was going right for me. It felt like the only good thing.

It felt like the only thing.

A new rebellious thought erupted: Could a doctor be wrong? Could I be right?

He coughed, breaking my thoughts. "You are not a homosexual. This is just part of what you're going through. I'm going to adjust your medications and we can see how you're doing next week. "

Time was up.

I remember this as the first time I ever doubted a medical professional. Because even in the ever-changing drugged up state, all of me knew that he was wrong about her, every tiny shard of my being knew that he was wrong about us.

I most definitely fall within the LGBTQ+ umbrella and outside the societal norm for sexual preference, gender identity, and relationship hierarchy (I'm demi-pansexual, non-binary, and polyplatonic which means I develop intimacy only with those I feel an emotional connection with, neither gender identity nor biological sex at birth matter to me, my own gender identity fluctuates daily with most days falling under the "agender" spectrum of feeling no gender, and that I have deep, loving relationships with many people). But I like to use the identifier "queer" which is a larger umbrella term for all of them.

I am still dealing with the aftereffects of this conversation today and will likely come back to the trauma of how I first came out again and again throughout this life.

My first queer relationship can only be described as a classic Victorian romance full of stolen glances, shame, pride, guilt, and an acute, sometimes glorious, often painful intensity. We held hands falling asleep in the same bed every night for over six months before we admitted we had feelings for each other. We invented our own eighth day of the week for how much time we spent awake through the middle of the night into the quiet mornings together, cherishing the time we had to be completely alone.

She was a blazing fire when I was close to freezing to death.

She looked at me and saw what I couldn't, and what I still sometimes doubt.

She saved my life in a real, tangible way.

She was eventually the reason I would flush all the pills down the drain.

And she set me on the track to becoming a scientist.

Whenever I'm asked about my trajectory into research, I struggle to describe this very early portion, because my memories of that swath of time are all fucked up. In fact, I don't have any memory of actually attending any classes for pretty much that entire year and change. But I know my brain was at least partially present because I remember the concepts I learned in those classes well enough to teach them later in graduate school.

All of my other adult memories are lined up on a little timeline in my brain that I can pull from and know when they occurred, often to the exact date. I don't have much memory of my childhood, but they are all definitely still in order, just with big blank slates between them.

But the time I spent on psychopharmaceuticals has my memories all jumbled. It's like they all happened at the same time, or maybe it's like they didn't happen at all? Some of them have an unreal, out of focus feeling to them, while others are far too sharp to not be reality.

In the very middle of this jumble of memories, I was forced to face the consequences of being queer. When my girlfriend's family found out about us... it was **bad**.

After over 72 hours of complete radio silence, a record for us since we first started holding hands every night for over half a year, I was scared and desperate when I received the text: "My mom found out... We can't talk anymore," followed by, "I might not even come back to college."

Gravity shifted and I was on the ground. She was my lifeline - a codependency that was unhealthy and led to an unhealthy response to her sudden removal from my life. Every cell in my body felt like it was an ember getting fanned into combustion, the hot air bubbling up from within as I tried desperately to tamp it down before I burst into flames.

Then it popped.

I was doubled over and screaming myself hoarse. The pain was everything - it was inside and outside. I yearned for physical pain to lessen the focus. I wanted to cut; I wanted to burn. I wanted to bleed.

I felt as if my insides had been slashed with a searing hot blade, and my skin was wrapped in barbed wire. I had learned very young that the conscious addition of physical pain from the outside felt good in comparison. It felt like the sharp pressure and burning on the outside leached the fire from within and the barbed wire retreated. And it felt reassuring to have direct control over at least a portion of what my brain was feeling.

It always stopped the further progression of my brain, at least temporarily.

But this had escalated too quickly and was too all-consuming. I was on fire, my brain an internal inferno, and everything I was thinking was already in flames.

After what must have been hundreds of unanswered calls and texts, I grabbed my keys to drive down to LA, the uncertainty eating me up. Maybe I would make it down there, maybe not. There was no shortage of cliffs down the coast of California.

"Hey Miyabe, hey, HEY! What is going on?!" My housemate banged through the door in the laundry room that connected my room in the garage to the rest of the house.

The laundry room and my room in the garage were several steps down, so I was caught choking on my tears while staring at her knees. I had been hiding our relationship from everyone for months. In the turmoil and tears, the whole story came spewing out of my snot-salty mouth.

I'll never forget how she looked at me. It was instantly clear that everyone I lived with had known the entire time, months and months before me.

It's still true that I'm often the last to know things about myself, a consequence of having fairly severe difficulties identifying my own emotions and delayed processing of all my social interactions. It can sometimes take me years to fully grasp something difficult, especially if there's an deep emotional component.

She grabbed me and held me with solid pressure, which only made me sob more violently as she said "Listen to me – you did what was right in your heart and there can never be anything wrong with that. Do you hear me? **You did nothing wrong**."

Those words still bounce around my brain.

I can still hear how much force and emphasis she put on the last part. I will never forget the solid, balancing feeling that cut through the pain and leveled me - at least momentarily - to think of something else. It was like getting a sharp slap in the face, but nicer.

It was the feeling of support.

But had I done nothing wrong? It felt like I had. It felt like it was all my fault. A lifetime of my natural instincts being incorrect and socially punished had shaped my default mode of self-blame.

"I'm going to take your keys so you don't drive until you've calmed down," she said as she went to make tea.

Left alone in my room, I rummaged through my junk drawer and found a clean-enough looking razor blade. I looked down, my right thumb was tracing over a small X-shaped scar on my left hand.

You should never do that to yourself... a distant memory rang out.

With what felt like the force needed to move a stalled truck, I pushed myself to standing and paced my room. My eyes lit on an option - a crumpled thin plastic bag with a handful of dry, popcorn-sized nugs (short for "nuggets" and used to describe trimmed cannabis flower). I packed my steamroller with everything that was left of my stash, about a half gram in all. With each cloud of smoke I exhaled, I felt the familiar veil wrap around my brain, smothering the fire back to coals. I felt the sharpness, the contrast of the day's events smoothing out to be more manageable, more comprehensible.

When all that was left was ash and char, I was no longer a danger to myself. The sadness was still there, but the sadness was always there. I still hated myself for loving her, but the uncontrollable magnitude of emotions had passed.

The internal inferno had been cooled to a duller, throbbing ache in less than fifteen minutes.

It's one of the most useful and most dangerous aspects of cannabis, that it dampens emotional intensity. In specific times, this can be therapeutic; it can be a reduction of harm to the alternative actions. But as a constant driving force it can lead to escapism, or running from problems instead of changing to face them. And it can be difficult to tell the difference, especially in a crisis, and especially if that crisis is a lasting, seemingly endless one.

Upping a dose for a more challenging stretch of time can absolutely be beneficial. But developing extreme tolerance also comes with consequences, so it's important for people to know their therapeutic minimum - or the smallest amount of cannabis necessary to receive certain beneficial effects. Different issues will have different therapeutic minimums and different people will as well. To make things more complicated, sometimes the therapeutic minimum can change depending on current stressors, global politics included.

I never even knew what a therapeutic minimum was until I had already been using cannabis for over 8 years. Before that, I was nowhere near the minimum; I was not even in the ballpark. And it definitely would have improved my experience to be more intentional with my medicine.

I ended up driving down through the middle of the night, chain smoking cigarettes out the window of my black 4-runner. I talked to my girlfriend on the side of the road, a block away from her house, and were immediately, inescapably re-ignited. We ended up secretly getting back together, living together, and hiding it from her parents.

After we moved into our apartment, I got my first medical card, causing my psychiatrist to label me an addict. It's a Shakespearian double tragedy and comedy that he diagnosed me as having a substance use disorder for cannabis when he prescribed me with the anti-anxiety medications that would be one of my most feverish addictions.

I hoarded them, always hanging onto them as a last resort, as my last way out if things got out of control.

I regularly mixed benzos (short for benzodiazepines, the most popular class of anti-anxiety medications including Xanax, Ativan, and Valium) with alcohol, which stupid and dangerous and almost resulted in an overdose. But I was chasing that sweet oblivion and it honestly would have been an accident.

One night during this black period I collapsed on my bed face-down and questioned if I had taken my sleeping pills, or if I had taken them twice for that matter. I flopped over onto my back as my body was sinking

sinking sinking downwards, like gravity had suddenly multiplied. It felt like a spinny ride I used to love at the fair where you are basically placed in a large centrifuge (a piece of laboratory equipment used to spin samples around very, very quickly which can separate out particles from liquid). But I wasn't spinning; this time it was the combination of drugs pulsing through my body immobilizing me and it wasn't going to stop anytime soon.

I could not lift my arms. I could not roll over. I couldn't even tell if I was breathing or not. It seemed like everything was very slow and very restricted. I was quickly fading out. There was nothing to do but succumb to it.

I had a single moment of panic, before a wave of acceptance as I let the blackness pull me under.

And when I woke up the next morning, I couldn't help but think, "in some ways that would have been a relief. It's too bad, really."

This is one of the most dangerous combinations of drugs out there, mostly because of the availability and accessibility of the molecules involved, but also because all three of them compromise short-term memory and decision making. Anti-anxiety and sedative drugs are some of the most commonly prescribed medications out there and, well, I don't think I need to go into too much detail about the integration of alcohol into our society despite its clearly poisonous toxicity profile.

It is a huge mistake to mix them, yet so many people do. Most of the time medical professionals and scientists speak about this from an incredulous point of view. I've encountered many passive, condescending tones when their lack of comprehension is on open display and being discussed over wine and appetizers, safe and secluded in the ivory tower of higher education.

I couldn't tell what was worse, the people who thought that we were stupid or the people who thought that we were poor, helpless victims in need of a savior.

"The warnings are so clear so why would they disregard them at the cost of their health? There must be something wrong with them that they can't stop. We should study their disordered brains so that we can better understand how to help them; we should find the molecular mechanism of their 'disease' so we can finally 'cure' it."

But I completely get it. I think it's simple, really.

Alcohol has a similar therapeutic profile to anti-anxiety and sedative prescription drugs, so the synergy created from combining them can seem overwhelmingly desirable, especially to those in crisis. Alcohol is one of the most powerful drugs out there and we take it in larger doses than any other drug.

The high from alcohol (both mind high and body high, which we call "being drunk") is intense. It's a dampener that can provide relief in the short term that overpowers the certain net negative it can have in the long term. And it is not just socially acceptable; it's encouraged.

When you combine this with the blissful nothingness of anti-anxiety medications, it's a momentary relief from what feels like an unending series of compounding stress, chaos, and pain. It's the perfect experience of drug-induced calm and carelessness and nothing else is that easy, which makes it a powerful medical tool but also powerfully rewarding, and in my opinion the most dangerous, especially for some types of neurodivergent brains.

Some brains like mine are built to run with that combination of routine and reward seeking.

But I don't see it as a disease or a disorder. I view it as a larger perceived benefit that is only felt by a specific neurotype, or a type of brain functionality, due to the increased stressful and painful circumstances experienced by that specific brain (caused by any number of factors).

The larger perceived benefit creates the larger reward. This larger reward is combined with other traits that can become vulnerabilities like enhanced pattern-recognition, which helps the brain to associate the drug with the very, very large reward and fuels its continued use. Then there's rigidity to routine, and drugs can become embedded within routines. This is actually encouraged for most psychopharmaceuticals and can be both a benefit and a detriment for all drugs. The real question is whether or not the person is experiencing a net benefit overall, or if the improvements in quality of life outweigh any negative effects.

The net benefit of the psychopharmaceuticals is always assumed to be greater than the risks, but we never give that benefit of the doubt to cannabis. The cloudiness of cannabis in the brain is always net negative, but the cloudiness of psychopharmaceuticals is part of their mechanism of action. The cognitive and memory deficits caused by cannabis can ruin the brain and make the user a stupid stoner, but the cognitive and memory deficits caused by psychopharmaceuticals are side effects that may come along with their positive effects.

The most ridiculous contrast between the two is the immediate toxicity. Cannabis is not acutely dangerous, meaning overdoses of cannabis do not cause death. There is no immediate route to suicide with cannabis. Having a prescription for sedatives and anti-anxiety medications was like putting a loaded gun on my bedside table.

But probably the gravest biased interpretation comes when medical professionals preach about cannabis making mental health worse. **Because the truth is that all of them are capable of making things worse, not just cannabis**. There are known correlations between many psychopharmaceuticals and increased suicidality and/or other routes of further intensifying a mental health episode. It is hypocritical to look down upon cannabis use when the same established risk exists for the synthetics.

My brain was tangibly worse when I was on synthetics. I was at my most volatile. I was at my most out of control. I was getting stretched thinner and thinner, so fragile I could hear myself breaking as every move I made caused cracking, my sanity leaking out at an ever increasing speed.

While I was on the prescriptions, my behaviors reached new levels and I started to be a shadow of myself. I started feeling like I was dying, but in an evaporative way, like I was slowly getting fainter and fainter until I would disappear and finally stop existing. In the glimpses of time I would feel myself again, I would get fiery compulsions to end the sad show in a faster and more efficient manner.

It took years of recovery for me to be able to reflect upon what happened, all of the drugs, all of the coercion, all the shaming. It took years of pharmaceutical research to begin to grasp it, years after my PhD to understand it, and years as a community advocate to accept it:

It was medical trauma.

It is without a doubt that psychopharmaceuticals are helpful and can save lives, but it is also without a doubt that some people do not respond well to them and would benefit from additional options.

I don't blame any of my doctors, nurses, or specialists. It's the system that's broken. No single person was responsible for what happened to me, myself included. I was a difficult and complex patient in crisis and I was burning through all my options.

Cannabis should have been an option.

Cannabis is almost always a reduction of harm.

There are risks associated with cannabis, yes, but there are risks to the alternatives as well. When we talk about cannabis use, most studies point to abstinence as the healthier option. Abstinence is the "control" group.

But abstinence is not always an option.

In a direct parallel, abstinence from sex is also the sure-fire way to not get pregnant or find an itchy bump in an unwanted place. But focusing on safe sex practices leads to less unwanted pregnancies and lessens the spread of sexually transmitted diseases, because abstinence from sex is not a real option for everyone. I mean, isn't it clear that one of the biggest abstinent populations has far too many direct links to pedophilia and child abuse (I'm talking about Catholic Priests)? Abstinence doesn't come without its own downsides, especially for neurodivergent populations.

If you apply that to cannabis use, abstaining typically doesn't mean abstaining from all drugs. It often means cannabis is replacing a different drug, most commonly alcohol, sedatives, painkillers, benzos, and other prescription pharmaceuticals. These all come with their own long term effects.

Some of them are so new that we don't truly understand their long term effects and most of them display at least some toxicity over prolonged periods of time. So for the significant population of people who will never be abstinent from all substances, the scales start to become tipped. People are pushed to use the most socially acceptable, legal, and protected substances rather than the best fit for overall balance.

And that balance could include lower doses of both. We regularly prescribe combinations of psycho-pharmaceuticals and there is plenty of lived experience of people finding relief from specific combinations that include cannabis. All the main arguments against including cannabis can be fixed by improving education, instruction, and intention.

Instead of preaching abstinence, I hope we can shift the focus to safer practices.

We need to immediately prioritize community education for safer practices for cannabis, because dosing and routine are not heavily monitored or controlled by a medical professional. And many people test the waters with cannabis far earlier than we want to admit. This does mean in some ways it can be riskier as a medicine - at least at the beginning when a large series of trial and error experiments are necessary to understand the relationship with the plant.

While we don't yet have "official" procedures for how to introduce people to cannabinoids in the path of least resistance, shouldn't we? Shouldn't we teach about titrating up, the act of slowly increasing a dose from sub-perceptual to full effects? Shouldn't we be providing public education on the benefits of balancing cannabinoids and practical knowledge like how to evaluate the quality of the medicine (the variability in quality and the difference in therapeutic effects is larger than almost all consumers understand)?

Shouldn't we be talking about how many of the risks are linked to overuse and extreme tolerance to the primary active cannabinoid THC (tetrahydrocannabinol), which is becoming heavily concentrated in legal markets?

Shouldn't we be talking about how every smoke sesh, dab, hit from a vape cart, or edible gummy is a dose that can cause both good and bad changes to our entire system?

We should.

And we should be building this knowledge foundation early like when we start introducing sex education.

If we don't start teaching children about it now, we will just end up with yet another generation of clueless adults. And the stakes are becoming much higher, because not only is the accessibility to cannabis increasing, but the strength of cannabis products are increasing. I believe that concentrated products like dabs and vape pens should be for more experienced users who have a better understanding of the intention of their use, not for teenagers to hit in the bathroom stalls at school.

The availability and ease of overuse of concentrates like vape pens and dabs gives me pause, especially when considering the introduction of cannabis to young teenagers. Though I started around the average age in my mid-teens, I had limited access to concentrates until I was well into my twenties. And the flower was weaker back then, too. Based on just the way the flower looked and felt, I'd estimate most of the bud I had access to was around 10-15% at most and that was plugged into the early Cali medical system.

Concentrated products are important and valuable medical tools, but they do come with a higher risk profile and it's critical to talk about it. Side effects, negative experiences, rapid tolerance, and withdrawal are all more likely to occur when regularly using higher doses. Some early signs of this can include anxiety, insomnia, lack of appetite, and nausea. And it's much easier to prevent the onset of extreme tolerance and withdrawal by backing off at the earliest possible sign than it is to try to weather the "cold-turkey" rebalancing after it's gone too far.

Advocating for the medical framing of cannabis at a young age could lead to safer recreational practices. Providing guidelines that include recreational use would open the potential for shaping use practices from the start as opposed to abstinence, which a significant population will just ignore (me and all my friends certainly did).

There is so much potential for using cannabis to be a route to developing deeper self awareness, intention, and direction.

There is so much potential for cannabis as a route to self-determination and agency in personalized medicine.

But changing this framework requires the existing medical system's participation and support. And another hard truth is that many medical professionals have no formal training on cannabis as a medicine and the critical role of the system in the brain that it activates, the endocannabinoid system. Continuing education courses for cannabis as medicine should be mandatory for practicing physicians in medical states. This is the only way they can revise the information they were taught during the prohibition to better serve their patient populations.

We need to gently teach medical professionals that they have been brainwashed by propaganda and the intentional manipulation of scientific interpretation of the pharmaceutical framework. The prohibition of cannabis (and psychedelics) coincided with the exponential development and heavy marketing of the new age of psychopharmaceuticals. Medical professionals were trained to associate cannabis only with criminality, and most are still unaware that medical cannabis was sold by several major pharmaceutical companies before they moved on to push more profitable products.

And despite the years of cannabis use, years of academic and industrial research, and years of community advocacy, most medical professionals will still push me towards those profitable pharmaceuticals. They can't help it, because they honestly believe they have my best interest in mind and that I am the crazy one.

Well if choosing cannabis over psychopharmaceuticals for its clear net benefit is crazy, then I'm not of sound mind and I never will be.

I am a biased scientist and I've spent a long time feeling lesser than for it. But all humans have biases; it is impossible not to. I've realized now that all scientists have a bias and those who are operating within the pharmaceutical framework (with all of their biases) just happen to have the major systems of power lifting them up and filling their pockets.

There are many like me who are silenced by the system, forced to restrain their opinions and hide their lifestyles in order to remain palatable to the funding powers of capitalism and colonialism.

It's just one example of all the ways in which we allow the pressures of the controlling tier of society to actively and passively control our behavior.

None of us are immune to it.

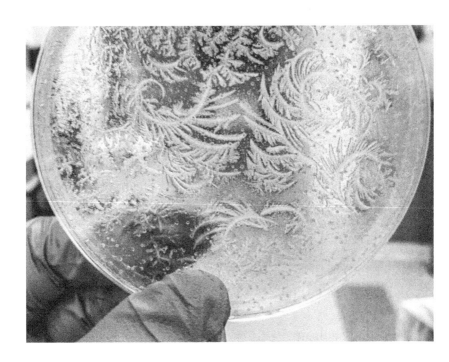

3. Bitten by the Lab Bug

"Have you ever thought of going into biochemistry research?" My professor asked in his pleasantly muffled voice. He had a corrected cleft lip that gave some of his words a slight slurring at the end.

It was comforting to me.

He directly addressed it in his first lecture and encouraged people who did not like it (some were already snickering and chuckling under their breath) to immediately drop his course or suffer the consequences.

I always admired that brazenness. He was one of the first of a long line of unapologetically different scientists I encountered that set an example for me.

"No, but I like the lab," I said as I looked at the wiry blue and white carpeting. I had only had about one week of clear thoughts at all; the decision to come off all my prescription medications was still fresh paint and subject to smearing

"I can tell you like the lab," he chuckled, "you should apply to work in one of the labs downstairs. What would you be interested in?"

"Drugs in the brain."

"Neuropharmacology."

Neuro - brain - **pharmaco** - drug - **logy** - the study of. The study of drugs in the brain.

The coolest root of them all is pharmaco which the Online Etymology Dictionary says is from Greek "pharmakeia" or "a healing or harmful medicine, a healing or poisonous herb; a drug, poisonous potion; magic (potion), dye, raw material for physical or chemical processing."

My favorite is magic (potion).

I took a classic mythologies course during my black-out period, which I think I really liked, but can't remember. My special interest in the Greek roots of many scientific words was something that stuck.

I was day by day remembering things about my own mind; I was learning to navigate again without the constant warping and shifting perspective of a psychopharmaceutical.

"There's an entire department for pharmacology and toxicology here. You should take a look at the noticeboard on your way out, because they each specialize in a core project." He said before starting to gather his papers, a sign that the conversation should be ending.

I grabbed my bag and headed down the stairs. When I reached the ground floor I glanced to the cork board on the left, feathered with postings. An emotion sprung up through the carpet and twined its way up to where it wound taut against my throat, but not in a bad way.

Years later I could identify it as the slightest bit of hope, a feeling I wasn't familiar with since being wiped clean of all feelings. The tightness wrapped around my body and squeezed all the blood to my brain. I took two steps towards it, before shaking my head, turning and walking straight out the door.

It was stupid to even consider it.

As I biked to my job cleaning the locker rooms at the pool, it started to drizzle and I let a little sob slip up my throat and felt the familiar burning in my eyes. Scientists are smart and good people, I thought to myself. A scientist can't be like me, all jumbled up in the brain with my holey memories.

A scientist wouldn't be so broken.

It was a nice dream, but I was way too fucked up to be a scientist.

That night when I opened my email, I had only one new message:

SUBJECT: Undergraduate Research Assistant Wanted

My heart skipped a beat as a fresh, cool wave of synchronicity washed over me, the hairs on my arm angling upward. It seemed more than coincidence after my conversation earlier that day and my brand new, secret, seemingly impossible dream of becoming a scientist. The feeling of synchronicity was more than coincidence, it was magical.

Some brains are more prone to mystical experiences than others. For me, the sheen and weight of significance of certain experiences can be impossible to ignore. My life is dotted with landmark mystical inferences that have a divine importance to me. They are moments when messages are being delivered to me and I cannot refuse them.

Writing this book was certainly one of them.

As a child, my Grandma Kinu told me it was a gift and that this power ran through the matriarchal lineage of our family (in their generation it was her and my Auntie Elsie who carried the torch). She encouraged me to discuss my experiences with her and would point out how helpful it was to be spiritually connected.

I would see my Grandpa Ume often even though he passed years before my birth. I felt empowered by it and proud of it. It wasn't until I started getting bullied for it at school that I learned to conceal it. It wasn't until it was labeled as hallucinations that I learned to fear it.

I lost that sense of mysticism in the black-out period (which makes sense, because mysticism can also be interpreted as delusion or grandiosity, symptoms of psychosis in western medicine that some of the prescribed pharmaceuticals I took are known to decrease). I had been told it was part of what made me ill, but it felt so undeniably good to have it back.

If feeling this right in my own body and mind was being sick, then I preferred being sick to the endless fucked up path towards being well (or whatever their idea of wellness for me would have looked like at the end of that road).

I opened the email and saw that the topic was eicosanoids and drug discovery. Drug discovery, that was exactly right, but I had no idea what the hell an eicosanoid was.

A quick search of the internet told me that they were signaling molecules that every human creates. They are fatty molecules, meaning they are made up of long chains of carbon, that help control inflammation and the immune system. And they were downstream versions of **endocannabinoids.**

WAIT WHAT?!

Endo - within or inside - **cannabinoid** - as in my favorite plant, *Cannabis sativa* (the scientific Latin name for weed, ganja, marijuana, bud, chronic, Mary Jane, reefer, etc)?!

Cannabinoids inside our body?!

Internal signaling molecules that we create are similar to cannabis?!

We make cannabinoids?!

Being introduced to the endocannabinoid system (also abbreviated as ECS) was like a kick to the gut; it knocked the wind out of me. Barely stopping to breathe, I verified that this system had been discovered from its activation by THC, the main active molecule in cannabis. The earliest trickling of understanding began to take shape from the deep fog of my brain.

The endocannabinoid system is a critically important system that all warm blooded life on earth needs to survive - actually evolutionarily there are ties all the way back to some of the earliest and simplest forms of life like hydra which are relatives of jellyfish.

It is everywhere in the brain and body.

It has been established as an important therapeutic target for a huge array of different issues (many of which were directly related to my experience of life). My eyes were glued to my computer as I labored through reading one of my first scientific articles, stopping every third or fourth word to look up the definition before moving on.

This must be it, a voice in my head rang out hopefully, this must be what is wrong with me (which later I learned was internalized ableism). I must have a fucked up endocannabinoid system and that's why cannabis helps me when all the prescription medications didn't.

I was filled with an immediate, reductionist, and linear certainty - I would figure out how to fix this system and I would finally be normal.

I would finally be acceptable in the eyes of society.

I learned that anandamide (abbreviated as AEA) was the endocannabinoid molecule inside my brain that had a similar mechanism of action as THC. And that it was linked to pleasure pathways and so was named with the root "ananda" which is sanskrit for bliss. This molecule went on to activate specific cannabinoid receptors in our brains - the same receptors that were responsible for the effects of cannabis.

My mind was blown.

There was hope for me after all, my whole body felt gripped in its vice-like hold.

When I found myself training to work in that lab a few weeks later, I felt guided. I felt like I was on the path to fulfilling my purpose. I felt like everything that had happened to me had reason; it wasn't just for the sake of my suffering. And I rode that initial wave of positivity all the way through the first half of my PhD.

I'm clearly biased, but I think the endocannabinoid system is the most important system in the entire brain and body.

It weaves itself closely knit together with all the other major systems - serotonin, dopamine, GABA, glycine, glutamate, opioid, endocrine, and more. While we like to think of these systems as separate, they are far from it. All of them share the burden of regulating the brain and body together and have intricate, complicated webs of control that they will exert over each other at any given situation; pulling the string of one always causes them to change at least one other. The tangle the systems weave is a semi-organized chaos.

But the reason the endocannabinoid system is so unique is that it's the only one that operates in a backwards direction from all the other neurotransmitters, a phenomenon called retrograde signaling.

Brain cells, also called neurons, talk by sending one another chemical and electrical signals, but only in one direction. The space between the two neurons is called the synapse and when two neurons are talking to one another across the synapse, there's always a talking neuron and a listening neuron. And the two never reverse. It's a one-way street.

The presynaptic neuron is before the synapse and is doing the "talking," meaning it sends the signals like dopamine and serotonin out across the synapse to the postsynaptic neuron that is doing the "listening," where receptors receive the signals that set off a series of domino effects on the inside of the postsynaptic, listening neuron. This series of dominos and all the buttons they end up pushing as they fall are what eventually cause the effects of a receptor being activated.

So two brain cells talking to one another would look like this: the presynaptic (talking) neuron releases a neurotransmitter (serotonin, dopamine, etc), the neurotransmitter crosses the synapse and docks at a specific receptor on the postsynaptic (listening) neuron, setting off a long chain of dominos.

But the endocannabinoid system functions in the opposite direction. The signals are created and sent from the postsynaptic neuron to the presynaptic, meaning the endocannabinoid system can send messages from the listening neuron back to the talking one and change the volume and frequency. This ability to operate in reverse is part of the reason the endocannabinoid system is essential to many core functions of complex life like energy metabolism, spontaneous brain activity, and the immune system.

It gives the endocannabinoid system a unique level of control over the other systems. In general, it's called "inhibitory," meaning in general when it is activated, it will decrease the firing rate or overall firing ability for the other brain cells it is talking to. The activation of the endocannabinoid system will generally quiet the other brain cells it's connected to. Since it stops them from signaling more, it's called inhibitory as opposed to excitatory systems like glutamate that will excite the cells and cause them to signal more.

Understanding the endocannabinoid system and the larger context of how much we do and don't know about the molecular mechanism of cannabis, especially how it's relevant for the neurodivergent community, has helped me to better respect and benefit from it as a medicine. It has made it a more reliable, replicable experience. It is absolutely a valid medicine for me and many others like me.

Cannabis really does dampen the unnecessary background noise bouncing all over and distracting me. And the quieting I experience might be caused by inhibitory effects of activating the endocannabinoid system on some other hyperactive or hypersensitive system(s). But it doesn't really matter if we have a verified molecular mechanism; almost all known psychopharmaceuticals still have relatively blurred theoretical molecular mechanisms.

Neuroscience is a fractal, the pattern only gets more complex the more we zoom in.

As technology evolves and we are able to look closer and closer at the underlying causes of neurodivergence, more and more detailed patterns emerge from what was before the blurred background. So it's no surprise that we are still finding new potential molecular mechanisms for existing psychopharmaceuticals.

Realistically this makes sense as many of them are not that old fluoxetine (Prozac), which is credited with being the first of a new type of antidepressant called "selective serotonin reuptake inhibitors" or SSRIs, has only been on the market since 1987, just 3 years before I was born.

Prozac is a millennial. And we certainly don't know WTF we're doing.

As someone who has been diagnosed with (accused of) grandiose and delusional ideologies, I think it was comically grandiose of pharmaceutical companies to brand and market antidepressants with a molecular mechanism when the field of pharmaceutical sciences was so clearly in its infancy. It's even more ridiculous that we still insist on calling them SSRIs when we know how dirty the drugs really are - they hit many targets and cause many, many other downstream or off target interactions. Recent publications indicate other systems are linked directly to their antidepressant activity, so how selective for serotonin can they be?

But they definitely do work for a lot of people. And they definitely save lives. And they definitely should be options for people.

They just shouldn't be the only option.

So all of this is to say that SSRIs are powerful and useful tools, but we don't really understand why they are working. The "serotonin theory" of depression has all but been debunked.

"The main areas of serotonin research provide no consistent evidence of there being an association between serotonin and depression, and no support for the hypothesis that depression is caused by lowered serotonin activity or concentrations. Some evidence was consistent with the possibility that long-term antidepressant use reduces serotonin concentration."

This is a direct quote from a big meta-review (a review article is a summary of known research up until that point, a meta-review is a larger type of review of reviews to get a broader perspective) by Joanna Moncrieff et al published in Nature in late 2022.

So after years and years and hundreds of millions of dollars of research, we're still operating mostly in the dark in terms of molecular mechanisms and drawing a lot of our conclusions from the existing activity of known substances. But I do get that saying "non-specific halogenated ether-linked double aromatic methyl amine" is way less sexy and marketable than "selective serotonin reuptake inhibitor" which has an implied scientific authority of its efficacy right in the name.

But the real question is if we should have ever allowed a profitable industry to define the different paradigms of illness when describing non-typical brain functionality when they were directly marketing specific molecules for those indications? It's way too late to question that, of course, but maybe it's time we re-evaluated it and took a deeper look at how that perspective has shaped the neurodivergent community's ability to have informed consent and self-determination with our prescribed and non-prescribed medications.

At the atomic scale, there is no known direct pathological link for most neurodivergent traits, only a long list of correlations. Or in other words, we have close to no idea how any of these systems operate and interact outside of a lot of generalizations and conclusions that are absolutely valuable and interesting, but ultimately were drawn with too many assumptions to be directly relatable to real-world experiences. And drugs function at the atomic scale.

For what it's worth, my real-world experience of truly believing that science said I was sick in the head was dehumanizing. It was the core of my self-loathing and a fixture of my sadness and suffering, because I wanted so badly to have a different, better brain.

This perspective was ingrained in me from the moment I entered the mental healthcare system and further solidified by my formal training as a scientist. Everything I learned was seen through the ableist lens of pathologizing neurodivergence, or categorizing atypicalities in brain function as a disease. Ableism and celebrating neuronormativity is deeply embedded everywhere in our society, but especially present in the ivory towers of academia, especially in specific circles of research (substance use, "drugs of abuse").

And I was blindly following that ableist path for a good chunk of my research career in an incredibly narrow-minded (and impossible) effort to cure myself by designing a new, synthetic cannabinoid pharmaceutical.

"Miyabe, do you want to go visit Hulahalla?" my research supervisor asked me. She was a young PhD candidate who was buttoning up her final years of her thesis.

She was the single most influential scientist in my career - in part because she's an excellent teacher who taught me to swim through the turbulent seas of biochemical research by pulling me in the shark cage with her, but also because as I recovered through working underneath her in the lab, we became friends.

We spent countless hours together alone in the lab talking about everything from formulating our osmotic mini-pumps to our personal lives and challenges. And as a friend who embraced both my atypical brain and my first queer relationship, she was the person who convinced me that I was capable of becoming a scientist.

The term "genius" was thrown around plenty in my childhood and young adulthood, but it was always a shallow evaluation. People who got to know me would add the very important descriptor "troubled" before it, then eventually as they *really* got to know me they would drop the original compliment and land on the very valid assessment of just "troubled" by itself.

But with the reliable access and better quality of medical cannabis, it seemed I was becoming less and less troubled.

"Yes! Let me just put these away," I responded as I finished snapping shut the caps of small plastic tubes and prepared to put the samples in the small refrigerator nestled under the standing bench. These samples would be taken to another building to be analyzed the following morning.

I loved that workflow (still do), I loved the technology and machinery (still do), and I loved the thrill of discovery (still do). I loved everything about research (do not still love *everything*).

"You're not going to believe it, but they said she is standing now."

I looked up at her in disbelief and she nodded at me as the electrical hum of the lab started to charge the air.

Just a few days prior we had gone to the stables to see the initial dosing of Hulahalla, a four-year-old thoroughbred horse, with one of the experimental anti-inflammatory drugs from our lab.

Laminitis is an infection and severe inflammation underneath the hoof, and Hulahalla had been lying in pain for days, maxed out on other pain and anti-inflammatory medications. The veterinarians were at a loss and beginning to consider euthanasia for humane reasons.

"Does that mean...?" I couldn't even say it. The serpentine feeling of hope began to twist and tickle its way up my calves. As the emotion grew to be more familiar, it felt less startling and strangling and more tingling. Hope was becoming exciting, uplifting even.

"It's really too early to say for sure, but they think she's going to make a full recovery."

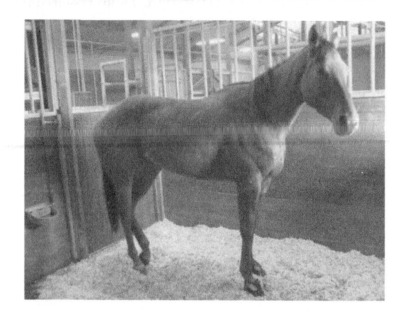

The first time I saw Hulahalla, a former racehorse, lying unmoving on a bed of straw, I saw myself - a washed out ex-athlete who lost their scholarship because they were no longer fit for competition.

Water polo had been a central feature of my life. I had been playing for years before me memory even begins. I started becoming pretty good at it, too, especially after I started smoking weed and eventually I was competing nationally and even internationally.

Since it's a team sport, it's no surprise that my increased ability to function within complex social systems improved when cannabis decreased my anxiety. Although I never actively medicated during competition, I was always at my best the day after a heavy session, and I benefited from decreased inflammation during recovery.

Since my early childhood, endurance exercise has been an important part of my regulation routine. My Grandma Kinu put me on a sensory diet, or a routine designed to help me stay calm throughout the day, by taking me to an early morning swim practice and evening swim practice starting when I was just 5 years old.

My brain is most flexible when my body is tired.

After leaving the competitive world, I found that combining a small dose of cannabis with exercise did help me enjoy it more. Later I would learn how much it makes sense that they would be complimentary given that the "runner's high" is linked to increasing levels of anandamide, which increases overall endocannabinoid system tone. But it took a very long time for me to rehash my relationship with exercise (and food). Being good at a sport was a big part of my understanding of my worth, especially in the social context. I had been forced to stop playing at the end of my black-out period - a retired racehorse.

When I saw Hulahalla standing again, I thought to myself, "that could be me, if I can find the right molecule." Which was really ironic because at that exact moment, it already was me.

I had found the right molecule, or molecules (plural) to more accurately describe it since cannabis is a combination of hundreds of different therapeutic molecules. I hadn't quite figured out the optimal dosage (the amount of drug to take) or dose schedule (when and how often you take a specific dosage), but I had found my medicine. I just didn't know it yet.

I was still too blinded by the stigma.

Cannabis was medicinal for me from the get go. But I couldn't fathom placing it in the same category as the prescriptions I filled so easily at the local pharmacy. I assumed (like so many) that cannabis was more dangerous, more harmful, and had less medical validity, which was why it was so stigmatized by most medical professionals.

False and false and false.

Cannabis is not nearly as dangerous as many of its alternatives, which is what makes it a reduction of harm from harder drugs like opioids and stimulants. It is one of the least toxic substances we have ever studied and has no known fatal dosage.

It's also far less addicting.

Can cannabis use become problematic? Absolutely, all substances have that potential (most people living in developed countries have a problematic relationship with sugar due to the mass profitability of our dependence on it). But in terms of physical and psychological addictiveness, cannabis is terribly weak in comparison to most other substances.

Hands down the most addicting substances I've experienced are benzodiazepines, tobacco (nicotine), and alcohol - in that order. And I'm extremely lucky my stomach doesn't hold up to the opioids or else I'm sure that would have made the list. If my cramping and constipation issues hadn't been so severe, the warm embrace of codeine was more than comfortable enough to cause me **huge** problems.

And even if cannabis use becomes problematic, the effects on the individual and their community is often less than a dependence on other drugs that would be more detrimental to physical health or more likely to induce violent behaviors. When comparing it to the crisis we are facing today with other substances, many of them introduced through pharmaceutical prescriptions or in the next grocery aisle over, cannabis is a clear reduction of harm and way easier to amend.

Emphasizing intentional, controlled, medical use of cannabis for chronic users can reduce this risk for overuse.

By far the biggest shift in my perception of cannabis as medicine came from learning about the endocannabinoid system and how many potential therapeutic routes have been investigated for a long list of things that cannabis has been shown to help with in human lived experience. The endocannabinoid system is one of the most powerful systems and can improve quality of life in many different ways, but three main domains of its control are mental health, chronic pain, and gastrointestinal (stomach and digestive) issues.

Gaining a deeper understanding of how cannabis works as a medicine completely changed my use patterns.

Activating the endocannabinoid system is ubiquitous, meaning it activates all over, because the CB1 and CB2 receptors that transmit endocannabinoid signaling exert control all over the body. The CB1 receptor is the most common receptor in the entire brain, and the CB2 receptor is essential to our immune system. And it's my opinion that many of the benefits of cannabis can be linked to this all-over activation as it can alter metabolism, or how our body manages energy, and inflammation, the very first warning signal in our complex immune system. But there are hundreds upon hundreds of different mechanisms of action that the endocannabinoid system has been demonstrated to exhibit through early research.

I hope one day everyone will know that there is a valid molecular mechanism for cannabis.

We have yet to completely, irrefutably, without-a-doubt prove these theories, but that is also true of virtually every other drug.

And science should never be irrefutable, because the entire foundation of science is built upon seeking knowledge that expands, and can often contradict, our previous assumptions.

We need to change this assumption about cannabis.

There is a valid molecular mechanism.

There is scientific basis for its therapeutic benefits, especially for neurodivergent brains.

4. Dosing Like a Scientist

*"Don't be afraid 'cause you know life's not for the weak
Or the incomplete."*

I felt the last vibrating notes ring out from my guitar as I opened my eyes and looked down at the red stone of my stoop. My whole body was tingling and hot, and my insides felt like a coiled rubber band wound tight. Before then, I had only let one other human on earth hear me sing and she was all the way back in California, a piece of me still with her.

My college sweetheart would eventually come to Boston, but after we had already outgrown each other.

It was devastating.

I am capable of great love. I like to swim in another person's soul and I like to feel their body so close to mine that I can't tell where I end and they begin. This is something I wouldn't change about myself, but it's also something that's made me capable of great loss.

She was a huge part of me becoming a scientist, but a lot of our relationship was spent in hiding. And a lot of the skills she gave me like how to dress and do my hair were incredibly useful to me professionally, but had a stifling effect on my true expression and interpretation of my own gender.

I was most feminine-presenting while we were together; I was a "lipstick lesbian" and performing femininity a lot of the time without truly understanding why. There were a lot of things I was still finding out about myself as I dove further and further into the abstract world. But in the first half of my PhD, my gender identity was still as unquestionable as my belief in the 100%, purely altruistic, good intent of pharmaceutical sciences.

I believed I was definitely female and Big Pharma is called that because their laboratories are so big, not because they have controlling, sometimes manipulative behaviors towards vulnerable populations. It was all simple and I was making my way towards my goal of being normal.

Research was my entire life and life was good.

I was rich in academic resources like fancy machines for my fancy experiments and I was looking into the molecular mechanism of my special interest. Nothing could distract me from how much I loved thinking about drugs at the atomic scale.

Learning so much about them for the first time was a thrill unlike any high I'd ever experienced; the research rabbit hole can be its own addiction and I was chasing that dragon at full speed. My experiences helped me color in the unfilled area between molecular theory and reality. I was always cross-referencing how the theoretical binding of the drug to its target in the brain created an experience.

Usually that target is a receptor in a specific system that transmits the signal of the drug to cause the effects. Different areas of the brain had different systems tangled together. I was only halfway through my second year and had already generated hundreds of theories about my own random experiences.

I was manic with all of my theoretical extrapolations. I was certain I would figure out how to cure myself. I was pursuing my PhD in the endocannabinoid system itself, working to understand the targets inside my brain that I wanted to modify. My hands were touching CB1 receptors. Surely I would find what I was looking for.

Surely I could find a way to live.

I was all energy, all the time. I spent every waking hour musing and processing all of the information - receptors don't always interact with a drug the same way, there are multiple ways of "turning on" the system. On top of that the separate systems are so far from truly separate. Our dogma of separating them out was more a result of the limitations of primitive technology and the early, simplified understanding of brain signaling. It went on and on and on.

I could hear my professors lecturing on repeat in my brain, little snippets got caught up in loops.

The tiniest of red flags was popping itself up. It was the first time I was somewhat aware of my altered state of processing. I both saw it, and couldn't see it. I was living too much for the abstract. It's why I turned to writing music in an attempt to tether me back to reality through feeling my body.

"Woah Miyabe, that was increeeeeeeeedible!" My mentor and friend commented from across the stone landing, "it's really emotional; it's really dark. I feel haunted."

We had connected over our shared perspective of science as a medium of art, just like water color or charcoal. He was a builder, a photographer, and a skilled biochemist. His desk in the lab was a curated selection of his favorite slices of ocean and forest views.

"Have you ever performed or played in a band?" He asked.

"No, I've barely played for anyone," I shrugged, still feeling some sort of discomfort, but definitely happy.

I picked up the half-smoked joint that was wedged next to the tuning pegs of my guitar and lit it up. The initial hit was ashy, but I puffed it twice quickly into my mouth to get the ember burning well, and the taste cleared up. I handed the joint over before starting to play a fingerpicking tune.

Before cannabis, I couldn't connect with music, but I was desperate to find it.

Musicality runs in my family. My grandma and grandpa played and performed as a musical duet together with her singing and my grandpa on rhythm guitar. My grandma once won a singing competition and got to represent the Big Island at the national performance;

she said that experience was one of the reasons her and my grandpa eventually moved to the mainland.

My mom was a violin savant - the first time she picked up the violin she could play it in pitch by ear. Her high school teacher was shocked and thought she was lying when my Grandma Kinu insisted she had never touched a violin before.

But I never took to music as a child. Even though I tried and tried and tried. It was very, very difficult for me to focus long enough. Even with my grandma playing ukulele side by side with me, I would feel my brain slipping away halfway through a song and stop thinking or switch to a different song.

And I didn't feel connected to the music. It was similar to how I felt about not being able to connect and make friends. It felt like I was trying to grasp it, but I kept finding my hands pressed up against the most frictionless glass barrier.

I think it was my inability to connect with myself.

I first started combining cannabis and music during my black-out period. Cannabis helped me be much more immediately present with creating music; it helped me channel some of my pain and suffering into a different outlet. Something clicked into place and the connection that was created went on to fuel the reorganization of

those past emotions into an expression that could be let out. This made every act of music impossible to lose focus on, because it became a form of communication.
It became the best way for me to speak to myself.

The more I studied drugs and how they caused therapeutic effects by altering the brain and body, the more I started to see music as a drug, one that combined very well with other drugs.

"You should definitely do a concert or at least go to an open mic! What about that violinist you were seeing for a while?" He asked tentatively.

"Laine?" I took in a sharp breath at the sharp and sudden stinging. "I still haven't heard anything..." It took all my willpower to ignore the pressing urgency, the panicked whisper at the back of my mind.

"Why not?"

"I don't know... I guess... something bad happened." I answered simply.

If my experience so far on earth had taught me anything it was that something bad was always happening, or about to happen.

The next day - in broad daylight on Commonwealth Avenue - I fell over two stories out of a tree onto the uneven concrete sidewalk, landing straight on my head.

I woke to every inch of my body in different types of pain. My arms were burning, my right knee was stiff and throbbing, and my neck and back were one giant, piercing ache that penetrated through to my ribs. I groaned, my breath coming in short gasps, as I rolled to my side and found my phone.

It was a cluster of panicked notifications.

One that stood out was a snapchat from Laine... Weird synchronicity.

It had been over half a year since we last spoke, and it had been a heavy, chaotic, confusing ending with no closure. I opened it. It was a selfie of him lying in bed wearing a dark blue and orange CitySport T-shirt with the caption "Sup" in an opaque text box.

I snapped a selfie of myself making a sad face, my arms covered in bloody scratches. "I fell out of a tree," I typed in the caption and pressed send.

And that was the beginning of my extra credit life and my marriage.

As I stared at the ceiling contemplating my next move, the night before came back to me in waves. A rush of guilt slammed into me - what had I put my friends through the night before? First I checked to see if the friends I was with had messaged me, they had, and they were worried. I sent them back a reassuring message about being in so much pain that I had to be alive before trying to sit up.

That was an immediate no.

Gingerly lying myself back down, I considered my options.

It was Sunday, so Urgent Care centers were closed... Damn. Living in Boston on my PhD stipend meant an emergency room visit wasn't in the budget (this wasn't the first time and would be far from the last time financial pressures affected my medical care; it's a reality of our broken system).

I looked down at my legs and saw my right knee was a dark patch of blood that had saturated through my green army pants. I must have already been in too much pain to think about removing them when I got home. Double damn. I knew all those trees would eventually come back to get me. I had already climbed pretty much every tree on the Esplanade, Common, and Public Garden; it was statistically likely I would fall.

I am the neurotype that leans into adrenaline - I like to go fast, I like to push limits. But this was something else entirely. It's likely my behavior would have been classified as mania, or a phase of extreme excessive energy, happiness, confidence, and impulsivity. I had displayed this category of behaviors during my black period as a negative side effect reaction to taking an antidepressant, I think it was escitalopram (Lexapro), but it might have been fluoxetine (Prozac). But this time there was no one to categorize me, so it's a gray area, like a lot of my life since I left the judgmental eyes of the medical system behind.

Mania can be difficult to talk about, because there is an additional implied instability or emotional volatility to people labeled as "bipolar" as opposed to just "depressed" or "anxious." It can undermine the confidence of that person to identify their own experience. It makes it easier to denounce deep emotions as temporary, passing, and a possible misinterpretation of either just the current high or low tide of the brain. It makes it more difficult to be able to tell if another person is manipulative, because having intense feelings and experiences devalued by others becomes the norm.

One of the things that fucked me up the most was how that label made me fear my own happiness. Every time a bit of joy crept in, I would begin to question its authenticity.

Am I really happy or is this a manic euphoria?

Am I really confident, because I'm a smart, focused, and able person who can accomplish my goals or is this a false grandiosity?

Am I climbing a lot of trees, because it's a lot of fun, or is it increased impulsivity?

I remembered climbing up the tree on Commonwealth Avenue, missing a branch, the disorienting feeling of gravity sucking me downwards, and then blackness. I don't remember the fall. My friends relayed to me later that I hit multiple branches on the way down before landing on my neck, then coming down hard on my knee on the corner of the sidewalk.

I was out cold for over a minute. That time for me felt both never ending and instantaneous. I was hovering over my body, slowly drifting further and further up and away, while I was a spectator to the scene unfolding before me.

I saw three strangers walking by gasp, one of the girls throwing both hands to cover her mouth. I saw my friends running towards my unmoving body; the shock and horror on their faces has been etched into my memory. It's a haunting reminder of the damage I've caused and am capable of causing to those who brave getting attached to me.

And then I felt the strong, sturdy presence of my Grandpa Ume holding my shoulders and he stopped my floating. With a small push I was sent back towards my body. And when I merged back into myself, I woke up.

When I came to, I was lucid and miraculously still able to walk. I was still drunk and somehow in the state we were all in, I convinced my friends to allow me to go to the Big D and the Kids Table concert we had been walking to. While at the concert I threw myself into the mosh pit, tagging people on the dance floor with my blood.

My general disregard for my own existence was so great that it wasn't until years later that I would be thankful I lived.

The Tree Incident, as I call it, is the most significant experience I have ever had, still sending me insights and messages in waves, years after its occurrence. It wasn't my first scrape with death, far from it, actually. I used to flirt with death, court it like a potential suitor that I would eventually succumb to. But this was the moment I finally decided against my lifelong assumption that suicide was an inevitable, uncontrollable force in my life that I would eventually fulfill.

It was clearly a miracle that I had lived, a gift from my ancestors, from my Grandpa Ume. I would be a fucking idiot to throw that away.

But the first moment I woke up, the only thing I knew was that I had to do something about the pain.

I needed to stop the inflammation from escalating.

I forced myself to a seated position and packed myself a full bowl. It was 10 AM in the morning, a proper wake n' bake. I pushed aside the encroaching guilt and shame, the feelings of worthlessness at needing to smoke in the morning. I was in too much pain to let my own judgment stop myself from seeking relief.

It's funny, at the time I had just learned about the daily cycling of endocannabinoid levels, but I still hadn't pieced together what that meant in terms of the importance of dose timing. I hadn't yet figured out that the morning was an important time for me to set up my day. I didn't understand that the morning was the most beneficial time for me to medicate.

Well, I did know I liked to wake n' bake, but I didn't know why I liked it. I didn't know that it was maximizing its therapeutic potential for me when my endocannabinoid tone was likely at its lowest, cycling to its highest in the afternoon just after lunch before dropping again.

At this point in my life I was still being thoughtless about my consumption.

I lit just the corner, so that as I continued to hit the bowl, I was at least hitting a little fresh flower for the rest of the bowl (unless it's a snap, I always corner my bowls). My overall pain subsided by about 25% - nothing miraculous, but enough to get me to stand and assess the damages in the mirror. I pressed all around my abdomen and other than the pain in my back and neck, there was no intense, sharp sensitivity.

I (stupidly) decided to wait it out until going to Urgent Care the next morning to save money.

I packed myself another bowl, decided to combine cannabis with another anti-inflammatory (ibuprofen, or Advil), and managed to shower. When I got out, my skin hot and pores open, I slathered my knee and neck with a cannabis salve made from coconut oil and shea butter.

Topical products like lotions, salves, and body butters are absorbed directly through the skin and deliver a larger concentration of cannabinoid molecules directly to the site of action. I've used topicals as a recovery aid for exercise, injury, and skin irritations and typically combine cannabis with willow bark which contains salicylic acid, the natural molecule that lead to aspirin.

The trick with topicals is to not be stingy - apply to a large area and reapply as often as the skin can absorb.

By the time lunch rolled around, I was in relatively good spirits. My friends brought me take out and we laughed about the ridiculousness of the entire situation over IPAs and pad thai. Years later, we would discuss it much more solemnly. The aftereffects of that day rippled out slowly and took time to build into substantial waves of change.

When I finally made it to Urgent Care the next day, nobody believed me at first, but once they did, I was a spectacle. Many doctors came in to examine me and I was told countless times to buy a lotto ticket. Somehow that hit me harder than anything just how close I had cut it. I was shuffled to different parts of the hospital as the tests went on and on.

It was in the third waiting room that I sent Laine a text asking to meet up to play music - the beginning of our musical duet as The Peppermints.

Laine changed everything for me.

Both of us brought previous baggage that made it painfully difficult for us to be together at first. And the beginning was a rocky transition colored with the same intensity, recklessness, and volatility of our individual pasts.

But we persevered through, because it was clear it was this or the continuation of the cycle (which likely would have resulted in death for both of us), and the support of another person facing and working towards the same goal facilitated both of our transformations. We slowly began to build a raft of stability. And from this stability, I gained the confidence to pursue something a little dangerous.

Both Laine and I loved pushing our own boundaries; it's part of what drove us together.

We were fearless.

We explored the corners of our minds with enthusiasm.

At first we both felt like we had nothing to lose, but as we grew more important to each other, as we shared more joy together, there suddenly became a lot there. I didn't want to stop having fun with Laine. I wanted to have fun with Laine forever.

But it was also clear that we were not on track to be alive long enough to make it to that next chapter.

The day I sprinted down Brookline Ave with Laine unconscious in a wheelchair from serotonin syndrome (accidentally mixing migraine medication with LSD) was the day I knew we couldn't create a future together if we didn't change.

I was screaming uncontrollably into my own knees in the emergency room intake cubicle, unable to process any of the things that were happening once they had taken Laine away. The nurse grabbed my forearm sharply, trying to get through, but I was already gone. Every inch of my skin was raw and felt like a bucket of hydrochloric acid had been thrown over me, I could feel the invisible blisters bubbling and popping.

"I think we might need the psych team down here, tell them to bring a sedative."

Wait what? My brain somehow had allowed that trickle of words to pass through and it was NOT an option for me. I would NOT be committed and put on prescriptions against my will.

I once had a panic attack during a travel trip for water polo and was forced by UC Davis protocol to go to the emergency room where they coerced me to take benzodiazepines. I never wanted that again and I definitely knew I didn't want to lose my individual rights to consent through the section 9 process of getting involuntarily committed.

"**NO!**" I managed to get out between sobs.

"Then I need you to calm down," she said sternly, then more kindly, "are you two together?"

I nodded.

"Well you definitely can't control who you love, but you can control you. You did the right thing telling the truth and once you've calmed down you can join your friend in the waiting room."

As I walked out into the waiting room in a fog, I felt an immediate responsibility to solve this as a scientist. I could figure it out; if I couldn't, I would definitely die trying. I knew then that the goal for both of us was the same: we needed to find a way to live with our pain.

And cannabis was part of that, but it had also become a source of doubt and questioning. Why did I need it? What exactly was it doing for me?

That next year I embarked on the most important experiment of my life - I completely eliminated cannabis for over 11 months.

It was not clinical. It was not controlled. It was not peer-reviewed. It was real life and it was messy.

I hope that sharing my story can help others who are similar to me better understand their relationship with cannabis.

I had never taken a conscious break from cannabis, ever (and I had been on the heavier side of self-medication). I wanted to re-evaluate its use as a medicine in the new context of my pharmaceutical training. My hypothesis, or my prediction, was that without cannabis, my "issues" would become more prevalent again. I could better identify them now that I had a deeper knowledge of how the different systems in the brain worked, and I could continue to modify my theories about the source of my own atypicality and how to change my life to meet it.

The first month and a half I assumed would potentially have withdrawal effects mixed in - I did notice I had difficulty sleeping, and a mild increase in my baseline anxiety. I missed cannabis a bit, but it was nothing compared to the other, more addictive molecules I had conquered (it took me three separate tries over six years to quit smoking cigarettes, I am still evaluating my relationship with alcohol after having been Cali sober for over two years, currently off any wagon, and I drink coffee every morning without fail).

An unexpected finding was that Laine almost immediately noticed my speaking affect, or the emotion/attitude displayed by my voice, dramatically changed (to this day, Laine can tell if I haven't used cannabis in around 48-72 hours by the way my speaking voice and intonation will change).

This is just one example of how helpful Laine (and their background knowledge in neurodivergent adults) has been to my understanding of my own brain. I had never before realized how much energy/thought I have to put into the way my voice sounds when I speak and never knew cannabis contributed to that one aspect of my ability to mask, or hide, my atypicality.

As the months moved along, the changes and new observations continued.

My sensitivity to sound ramped immediately and was noticeably peaking by the end of month 2. Certain sounds felt like a steel rod piercing through from ear to ear, and others like a coarse sandpaper was rubbing at my brain. Little background noises in the lab became impossibly distracting to the point that I started needing to wear headphones at all times when I was working.

During the first year of my PhD I had learned about a process called sensory gating, which is how the brain filters out background information like light, sounds, smells, and physical pressures. It's been pretty well-researched in its relationship to schizophrenia. I had theorized then that my brain had a lowered gate, meaning more sounds got through, but this theory would evolve to encompass much more than just my sensitivity to loud noises.

There were so many little things about myself that fell into place during this year. Like I always knew I preferred to bike as my main mode of transport, but it wasn't until month 3 that I understood it was because I am very sensitive to motion sickness. My vestibular system, which is responsible for understanding how our body is balancing and moving around, must be affected.

I remember as a child always feeling sick in the car and how as an adult I always prefer to drive because it minimizes this sickness. It never crossed my mind that cannabis was helping with this, but it certainly helped me commute on the T, Boston's rapidly deteriorating public transportation system.

As the motion sensitivity returned, I felt nauseated after only one or two stops and would sometimes need to get off the train in a rush and walk the remaining distance. It was luckily springtime when this effect began to seriously affect my quality of life, so I was able to move to biking and walking and continued the experiment.

Month 4 brought up a similar insight, but this time it was about how my brain perceives my body in space, or proprioception. I've always been excessively clumsy. I bump into many things as I go about my day, finding spare bruises mostly around my legs and arms. The lack of cannabis in my brain increased this ten-fold.

I started to loathe the grocery store, public sidewalks, and the library - my shoulders always seemed to find some other human to bump aggressively into. Spaces with more than ten people in it became overwhelmingly stimulating. And I started walking my head into a lot of things. I misjudged tree branches, stood up into overhead lights, and knocked the side of my head on street signs.

It's been proposed that some neurodivergent brains benefit from self-stimulating this proprioceptive sense by a repetitive movement, also called stimming. For me this was pulling and touching my head and hair. It's always felt like scratching an itch on the inside of my brain, and it's always there, but the lack of cannabis was making my brain itchier.

After a while my sound sensitivity changed to incorporate a different aspect. I started getting sounds "stuck" in loops in my head. This persists when using cannabis, but it's far more in the distance and benign. Words and phrases from movies or TV shows would pop in on repeat, demanding attention. I would hear a bird call that would "stick" for the rest of the day and I'd be surprised to hear it blasting through my brain while I was in my apartment cooking dinner - which can also be interpreted as an auditory hallucination.

My obsessive compulsive tendencies and paranoia returned with a vengeance around month 5. Before leaving the apartment every morning I would touch all the burner dials on the gas stove and say "off, off, off, off" as I toggled them to make sure they were indeed off. I would walk to the door, forget something, turn around to grab it, and go back to the door only to be compelled to return to the kitchen to repeat "off, off, off, off." I would sometimes grow paranoid in the middle of the day and sprint home on my bike to repeat this process, never once were any of the burners left on.

It was about halfway through the experiment that I started to seriously doubt the "magic bullet" approach.

Over a hundred years ago, the term "magic bullet" was coined to describe a single drug that can cure diseases by hitting a single target in the body. This has been the foundation of pharmaceutical drug discovery since then. We have dedicated a huge amount of energy and resources towards identifying the source of issues within our bodies which has helped us tremendously and lead to major leaps in human health. But some issues remain enigmas, mental health is one of them, and it was becoming clear to me that my mental health was critically linked to many, many factors, each with their own biological targets.

It was almost as if there was no single cause of these very different, but interrelated issues. Or that there was a single cause and it was that my brain processes the world around me in a different way (but that we don't fully understand what that means yet at a molecular level). And that it certainly wasn't just one single chemical imbalance to be fixed by a single magic bullet.

(And on top of that, I never liked the imagery of a magic bullet in the brain)

By the end of the experiment almost a year later, I was

S
  L
    I
      P
        P
          I
            N
              G .

I was struggling to find regular sleep; I was too afraid of what the night held. When I finally managed to close my eyes, I would shoot awake in the early hours of the morning drenched in sweat and gripped with terror.

I swallowed my morning coffee despite the nausea from the baseline anxiety and forced myself to go about my obligations. My body and joints began to ache too much for me to be physically active, so I stopped working out. All the noises were too loud, my clothes were scratching and itching me all over.

Everyone's eyes felt like tattoo guns raking through the inside of my skull. I didn't want to be around people. And I was drinking way too much to try to dull it all.

At a holiday party, I was gifted a head massager - its thin, long, needle-like legs still send shivers down my spine. Everyone who tried it seemed very pleased, so when it was my turn I thought nothing of it.

!!!!!!! WHAT THE FUCK !?

Each small metal wire felt like it was burning hot and tracing a line like lava across the top of my scalp. I screamed and dropped myself to the ground reflexively to escape the torture.

I can feel the lava on my head when I even look at that type of head massager. I can feel a prickle on my scalp right now just thinking about it. We laughed it off at the party, but at home Laine and I discussed what it meant about my growing sensory hypersensitivities.

Later that same weekend we were with two of our friends who we like to call our husbands, and I knew it was time for the experiment to end. Our ritual of these past eleven years has been to go into weekends with no plans and no judgements. Being together, just the four of us, has been one of the safest spaces I have ever known and are periods of great reflection and recovery, little glittering spots of hope floating in a pretty murky and desolate sea of memories (at least before the experiment).

Lying on their green carpet, I was worried that I had gone too far, because I didn't even want cannabis anymore, I wanted more alcohol even though I was over five drinks deep. I was dying for a benzo. And I had started smoking cigarettes again two months prior.

It was probably the surest sign to me that cannabis could be utilized in a responsible, regulated manner (at least in contrast to some of the other more available drugs). To this day I can't roll spliffs, and have to carefully monitor my blunts, because I am prone to easing my way back into cigarettes.

As we descended into the basement, I reminded myself of the whole point of the experiment. These friends put peppermint oil in their bong water, and stack ice in the neck above the ice catcher, so the smoke felt cool on my throat. I felt the cooling relief seep all the way into my brain as it was swept away into an immediate quiet that I hadn't felt in almost an entire year.

"So then what is the point of all this research?" I asked, exasperated, as I threw myself into a wired metal chair, the pattern biting into the back of my legs until I shifted my weight forwards onto my feet.

"To help people," said my friend from Journal Club, a weekly meeting of the pharmaceutical sciences PhD students where we critically analyzed research with a panel of professors. She leaned heavily into the seat next to me and sighed into the high ceilings of the lobby.

Our labs were all the way across campus from one another, but we often found time after Journal Club to take discussions further. She studied a brain growth factor associated with neuroplasticity, or the brains ability to change, and she shared my obsession with taking the theoretical science and applying it to the real world.

She continued, "and of course to make money. It can be both things."

"I don't understand that part," I replied. "One has to be the priority, which makes the other one irrelevant."

I had started to question why research always pointed towards more synthetic, pharmaceutical pathways rather than the potential natural method when the evidence pointed to both as different mechanistic options. The answer almost always came back to money, to patentability (or the ability to patent a molecule so that only one company, usually a pharmaceutical company, can sell it to make money for twenty years).

Natural medicines cannot be patented.

"It's not ideal, but research is expensive, especially our level of research. What other options are there?" She stated matter-of-factly. I really liked this about her perspective, she was a straight shooter. "I've been thinking about what we talked about last week, about how a combination of many weaker molecules might have unexplored therapeutic benefits over one super strong synthetic derivative. Are you thinking of shifting into natural medicines?"

I took in a sharp breath. Should I tell her where the idea came from? Should I tell her about my experiment?

The night I ended my experiment I smoked as much as I wanted, what scientists would call an "ad libitum" dose schedule, which roughly translates from latin to be "as much as pleases." But after waking up feeling fantastic, feeling changed, I decided to continue the experiment by intentionally dosing myself with different ratios of the two primary cannabinoid molecules found in the plant: cannabidiol (CBD) and THC.

While THC has long been championed as the most important molecule in cannabis, it was only due to its ability to alter perspective and lucidity. Recent evidence was showing that CBD had just as much, if not more, therapeutic potential with a minimal perceptible change in brain state.

My life changed dramatically when I discovered medicinal hemp. Hemp cannabis is any cannabis plant that contains less than 0.3% THC by dry weight, and for a long time hemp was used only to create fabric or hemp seeds for food. Once the farm bill changed hemp's designation, medicinal hemp types had emerged that were high in CBD (and now other rare cannabinoids) while remaining low in THC. It was a major win for medical cannabis in general, because it jump started an entirely new chapter of accessibility to the public to potentially more therapeutic molecules of cannabis.

I dove into the theoretical world and historical context of CBD's potential; the most notable finding was that CBD, which is often mislabeled as non-psychoactive, had significant therapeutic potential in the brain. CBD's powerful ability to stop seizures intrigued me; many prescription medications for seizures have overlapping indications for sleep, anxiety and mood stabilization. I wanted to figure out how much CBD and THC was necessary for specific effects and played with different ratios. I wanted to figure out the proper dose and dose schedule for myself.

And after just a couple months, the experiment had already paid off big time.

There are multiple ways CBD changes the CB1 receptor and this can affect the way THC feels; it can also reduce negative side effects of THC like anxiety and long-term cognitive effects. On top of that CBD interacts with other systems like the serotonin system (I would argue the primary target of CBD in the body is the serotonin 5HT1A receptor). By always balancing with at least equal amounts of CBD, I gained much greater control over the anxiety side effects of cannabis which kept my overall tolerance relatively low.

This also saved me a lot of money.

It turned out that I didn't need large doses, what I needed was consistent doses.

"Maybe... so, you know how the big downfall of natural products is that nature can create infinitely complex chemistry, every time, and that this variability leads to increased risks to benefits profiles? Well what if that risk could be reduced by optimizing for reproducibility, not potency."

She adjusted her head scarf absent-mindedly, I had noticed it was something she liked to do while pondering a new idea. "That's true. But it's hard to argue that optimizing for reproducibility could happen before stabilizing the chemistry of the plants themselves. And then there's the real big issue with natural products in that there are lower compliance rates in the consumer market and, I mean, dosing is everything."

Another harsh truth. Dosing was everything.

Being more consistent with how much and how often I used cannabis was what gave me reproducibility, meaning the effects were less and less unpredictable. This is an important metric of all medicines and cannabis can fall short on this without a lot of intentional control over what types of cannabis are being used, how much, and how often.

It shocked me what a big difference it made for me to apply just the smallest amount of effort into tracking my consumption with intention.

On top of that, this reproducibility and routine was helping me gain more and more certainty in my relationship with cannabis as first and foremost a medicine. With hundreds and hundreds of unique molecules in every cannabis plant, it could never be a "magic bullet." But that fact was exactly what made its therapeutic value so vast and diverse, why cannabis was able to help with so many different things. I had gone over the theoretical binding again and again, and come back with the same conclusion every time: no synthetic pharmaceutical could replace this for me.

And even if one day a new synthetic cocktail of hundreds of molecules somehow made it past clinical trial, I would never, ever, ever, ever, ever, ever, ever, EVER, EVER, EVER even THINK about trying it. I wouldn't consider it for one second. I would read the literature behind their reasoning and send positive thoughts to those experimenting with their minds.

And if it worked perfectly, that would be fantastic. It would be ideal for there to be a pharmaceutical answer to every issue. But even in that world, cannabis should still be an option. And back to reality, it should be definitely an option in our current world with so many chronic issues caused by uncontrollable inflammation with little to no options.

I believe cannabis should be the first line drug for anything that flares with stress and inflammation (ideally paired with switching to an anti-inflammatory diet).

Keeping systemic inflammation at a minimum can have beneficial effects all over the body, and almost every health issue we are facing in modern times can be traced to excessive inflammation. Cannabis is one of the most powerful and least toxic anti-inflammatory medicines and many, many people with chronic issues find lifelong relief with it. And these benefits could be even further optimized by teaching people how to develop their own personal dosing routine.

"But if those same consumers understood the full seriousness of dosing, maybe they would change their behavior," I was starting to feel an energy run through my bones. I was finally feeling strength in my opinion on my cannabis use. I was finally feeling like I understood myself. And I wanted to give that to everyone else like me. As medical cannabis became more and more commonplace, I wanted to make it the best possible medicine for everyone.

"Maybe they would care more if they knew more. And then maybe they would be able to find a regular schedule that works for them. I mean, almost everyone drinks coffee in the morning, but there's a lot of personal preference there. And most people who are sensitive to it know not to drink it after a certain time in the afternoon or end up switching to tea or giving up caffeine entirely. That was all trial and error."

"Maybe if they all got their PhDs," she gave a small laugh, then grew more serious, still pulling at the fabric against her cheek as her mouth set into a grim line, "but for the things I know you're interested in, the pharmaceutical framework of drug discovery is embedded too deep. It took both of us years understand its reach, and we are literally training in it, getting paid to study it as our job. Most people won't be able to think about it this much at that level; the barriers to accessing the information are just too high."

5. Falling From the Ivory Tower...

I was alone with the bartender in the basement of a hotel in Poland watching the sweat drip off my gin and tonic when one of my professors from Boston sat down next to me and ordered a drink.

"You're not going to go to the closing ceremony?" His raspy, heavy Swedish lilt once puzzled me, but after three years of group meetings and his course on Behavioral Pharmacology that was packed with interesting cannabinoid-behavior tidbits, I didn't miss a word.

He had a habit of going into personal stories that tied into his research at the time, which helped keep my interest, because he would drop in random tidbits of knowledge along the way. It was during his story about how he moved to America for love - an iconic counter-culture, international, cross-country roadtrip love story - that I first learned about cannabis causing hypothermia, or a decrease in body temperature.

Induced hypothermia is one of the main laboratory tests done to determine if a molecule is or is not a cannabinoid. If a molecule activates the endocannabinoid system at the CB1 receptor, like cannabis, body temperature will drop. Cannabis induces hypothermia.

This was a big deal for me, because that was a side effect that had gotten a lot worse after using the psychopharmaceuticals. And I wanted to fix it, because it wasn't pleasant to be cold and shivering, especially in New England in the wintertime. I had found that it was linked to high THC and hyper-dry flower - the crusty, hard, condensed nugs.

It was only one out of hundreds of little factors of my cannabis use that had been improved upon by learning more about the underlying system it interacted with. This conference was the very first time I saw cannabis research ever presented, and I was still reeling from all the information I was taking in.

I knew I wasn't supposed to be in the basement, that I was supposed to be in the main hall instead. After trying unsuccessfully to force my mouth to make the word yes, I settled for saying the only thing that was true, "I don't know if I'll go."

The ice in his drink clinked lightly as he took a sip and asked, "It isn't what you expected?" He half-laughed, half-coughed. I couldn't tell if he was talking about the research conference we were both attending, or if he meant something even broader.

Because entering into my fourth year of pharmaceutical research, none of it was what I expected.

I expected becoming a scientist would give me more certainty, not less. I expected to be finding answers, not creating even more maddening questions. And I expected to feel like I was helping in some way, not like I was a cog in a giant wheel that squashes all who oppose it.

"No, it's not," I sighed, "I don't know why I'm doing this."

I couldn't understand the existing dogma, or current scientific assumptions that everyone in a given field is supposed to use as the foundation of their interpretations for their research. The central dogma of pharmaceutical sciences is that stronger synthetics will eventually cure all complaints. It wasn't that I no longer believed in synthetic drug discovery; I absolutely did and still do value what that pipeline has created. But all the energy in my brain, body, and spirit made me feel that we should shift our focus. Because stronger synthetics will eventually cure some complaints, but optimizing natural products could eventually cure everything else (or prevent many of those complaints from getting severe enough to need synthetics in the first place).

I couldn't ignore the pressing feeling that we needed to be investigating the chemistry of life and I couldn't handle the generally agreed upon devaluation of natural medicines in my field, a perspective that reeked of both capitalism and colonialism.

My brain has never allowed me to expend energy on things that didn't make sense; it just turns its focus down a different road and I'm forced to follow. And searching for more synthetics when we had barely put any effort into optimizing the existing medicines wasn't making any sense to me. Plus the entire scientific system, rich and overflowing in resources, had been working towards that goal (and is still working towards it today), so my efforts would hardly be missed.

But I was completely lost. The only thing I knew for certain was that I did not want to work anywhere near the drug discovery pipeline. Including the seed of the system: academia.

"You love the unknown." His statement cut to the point; it was the only thing that I still believed was true. "And you'll never be satisfied unless you continue to look deeper and deeper."

He was right; I wasn't satisfied. By eliminating cannabis and reintroducing it slowly, I had expected to learn about the plant, but I ended up learning about myself. It resulted in the most positive relationship with any medical professional I have ever had - a psychologist who fully embraced cannabis and who saw me on a spectrum I never even considered for myself (it took over two years after his initial diagnosis for me to fully understand it).

And I couldn't ignore the mystical gravity that was pressing me to continue delving even deeper, to keep looking, even though I didn't know what I was looking for.

I was certainly still finding things, just not the kind of things I was used to thinking about. Because the more and more I discovered about myself, the more and more I realized just how much I was being forced to hide myself, to conform to the expectations of others. Despite being a community built by neurodivergent people, the roots of academic science, especially as it pertains to mental health, was founded on elevating and promoting neuronormativity, or the idea that there is only one ideal type of brain and person. And there was so much privilege involved in climbing the stairs of the ivory tower; it made me feel disconnected from reality with every step I climbed.

I started heavily investing my time into organizing and participating in student groups that built community support. It wasn't a smooth road. I had to file a Title IX complaint for speaking openly about my marriage, and was escorted off campus by armed police while tabling for the LGBTQ center. I grew cynical. I was losing sight of what I loved about science, because I couldn't separate it from the systems of power that nurtured it in exchange for how it could be manipulated to frame messages to influence the general public.

The scientific bias has been weaponized against cannabis for decades, and the superiority of single molecule pharmaceuticals over natural products is embedded even deeper within the dogma, going back hundreds of years.

"Yes, but I don't want to be forced to see from thieir perspective!" I blurted out in frustration, "I want to be able to explore all the possibilities without having to obey all this old baggage that everyone assumes to be true just because it was done fifty years ago when technology was ancient and science was only done by the privileged few who controlled the major opinion. And I feel like there's no way around it!" I felt the small sting of tears beginning to well up. But I knew they would pass and I wouldn't cry. Another perk of consistent cannabis use was that it placed me below my threshold for that particular situation of emotional control. There were still bouts of crying, just less publicly.

He considered what I said for a long time before speaking, very slowly. As the words traveled to me through the still air, I could feel the heaviness of each word as it reached me. "Well there is only one thing you can be completely certain of in this life." He stood and drained his drink, slamming it down ceremoniously before continuing, "No one will do it exactly the same way you will, so... you will just have to try."

The grand staircase just outside the bar was well-lit, so he was framed in a glowing light as he walked out through the double doors. My breath held in my chest as wave after wave of oceanic boundlessness washed over me.

I followed him through that light and went to the closing ceremony where I was shocked to receive a pre-doctoral research award for my thesis work with a new, upcoming endocannabinoid system drug target. As I stood at the front of the room with the other award recipients, I looked out at the sea of circular tables covered in white cloth, each one surrounded by renowned cannabinoid scientists from around the world, many of whom had dedicated their life to researching the intricacies of the endocannabinoid system. It was a community that I idolized, and that my heart ached to find my place in, but that didn't see my medicine (or my brain) the way that I did.

I didn't want to have to hide myself and the true intentions of my research interests. I didn't want to feel ashamed anymore. And I didn't know what that meant for my future.

But I did know that I would finish my PhD and go from there.

I hope we can become more aware of the presence of Big Pharma in both our research pipeline and our perception of all drugs.

I teetered on the edge of dropping out for almost the entire fourth year stretch of my dissertation. The mystical nature of that one conversation in a dark basement bar in Poland was my sign to keep going. I can't ignore signs like that, but I chafed more and more as my opinions deviated from the currently accepted dogma. I was angry and disappointed.

When I emerged from my black-out period during college, keeping my head above water was still a struggle. I found science as a life raft and I clung to it with all my might, allowing myself to be reeled onto a much larger ship in the process. But once I started working amongst the crew, I realized more and more that I didn't agree with the direction of the ship, even if it had saved me.

I couldn't come to grips with the pharmaceutical research mentality; I couldn't accept how clearly biased towards patentability and profitability the entire workflow was. It ate at me day after day how many millions upon millions of dollars were spent in that pursuit, how the interpretation of the results were subject to the same bias.

I felt like it might be worth the risk of drowning to be able to swim in my own direction. And I was devastated by the decision, because I had placed all my faith in a false idol.

Of course I had heard of "Big Pharma" before going for my PhD in pharmaceutical sciences. But I really did think that "Big Pharma" meant their laboratories were physically large - like that the buildings were huge and hundreds of people worked there (which in my defense, is true... they do have lots of big buildings and an entire upper echelon of society upholding their position of power). The connotation of "Big (Bad) Pharma" went way over my head. But this is just one of hundreds of examples of small misinterpretations or assumptions that seem terribly obvious to others that I just don't pick up.

My Grandma Kinu used to say, "you have to be careful because you are so smart, but you have no common sense."

So I dove headfirst into pharmaceutical sciences believing it was completely altruistic and all research was done with the sole intent of improving patient quality of life. I believed all drugs that made it to market were safer and more efficacious than any other known alternatives. The prioritization of profits of the company over that intent or any role of money in the pursuit of healing people wasn't an option I even considered.

But the extreme profitability of prescription medications that can be protected by patent has created a financial incentive for chemical farming over the study of optimizing the natural alternatives and preventative options. Even though the base structure of most drugs come from natural sources, most research on natural products focuses only on identifying new potential scaffolds, or a starting structure that goes on to be changed into something synthetic that is patentable.

Just a couple hundred years ago, before the discovery of receptors, before the boom of synthetic pharmacology, we had thousands of years of evidence for medicines that coexisted and coevolved with us. The lack of prioritization of investigating these known medicines and the insistence that they are lesser than their super powered up synthetic alternatives is a conscious choice.

It is a decision that is driven by the funding of the research.

It's undeniable to me that there are unexplored benefits to complex combinations of weaker molecules in natural products and crude (unpurified) extractions that cannot be replicated by single molecules. It's highly likely that the standards we have been using to develop the "good drugs" have been skewed by our ability to market those same "good drugs." And it's very possible that if we had dedicated as much time, power, and resources to exploring and integrating natural medicines into our healthcare system that we wouldn't be in such a dire state now.

When I found out that healing was the secondary goal, it broke my heart.

Part of me thinks my naivety could have been a self-protective delusion, that it was something my brain cooked up so that I could skip over processing what had happened to me as a result of this exploitation. But it feels more like just something else I've missed... like all the hundreds of other things I've missed that are under the big umbrella of social interpretation.

I honestly went into my research career believing I could create a synthetic, pharmaceutical version of cannabis that would be a better medicine. But all my experimentation - both in and out of the lab - led me to a different conclusion. I had found what I was searching for, it just wasn't what I expected. With my modified routine (low doses in the morning, higher doses at night, balanced with CBD) cannabis became a more reliable medicine for me. I found that cannabis was the better medicine.

During the final year of my dissertation, I was chosen to participate in a fellowship at MIT that included most major research universities and hospitals in Boston as well as local professionals from biotech startups, pharmaceutical companies, and PR and marketing firms. The goal was to maximize the impact of research, but I couldn't help but think about what it meant for the impact of my life in general. There was no shortage of ideas for what I could research next, but I was feeling detached from the academic community. Years of hiding myself were wearing my mask thin.

I wanted to be able to help others like me, but I wasn't ready to talk openly about my cannabis use. I didn't believe in myself as a role model, because... well... I still felt too fucked up. I was still grappling with my own neurodivergent identity. I knew I didn't want to hide any longer, but I wasn't confident enough to face the consequences of coming out (again).

I needed a completely different life. I was craving a sense of belonging and creative purpose and I found it as music teacher for high needs neurodivergent adults.

"My students have taught me more about my own brain than I ever could have imagined," I said tentatively into the microphone.

It was standing room only at the Hard Rock Cafe in downtown Boston for our music non-profit's end-of-session celebration concert. The lights pierced through the tops of my eyelids as I stared at the shiny black stage. I forced myself to look at the audience, a beautiful ocean of neurodiversity.

It had been two and a half years since Laine and I haphazardly decided to start our own 501c3 non-profit, creating a board and filing the state and federal paperwork in a manic blunder. We were supporting this endeavor with Laine's career as an accessible education teacher, my measly wages as a music teacher, and random wedding and bar gigs as a violin/guitar duet.

It was definitely a struggle, and the growth of the programming was supported by Laine and I volunteering all of our time as administrative officers. But we were proud of how far we had come. We had just opened our first music studio after being displaced from our first community location (the location is geared towards teenagers, and our mission was for adults).

"I used to be scared of what it meant to be different," I paused, the words getting stuck in a muddy puddle behind my lips. I couldn't figure out what to say next, the start of a communication block was forming. My heart lurched and I searched the stage for Laine in a panic, finally finding his calming forest-green gaze. Laine gave a slight nod and his serene presence was all the co-regulation I needed to continue, "but witnessing all of the explosive joy, the endless laughter, and the brilliance, the miraculous events in our community has completely erased that fear."

I briefly glanced across the stage at all of our music students with their instruments, ready for our grand finale performance, so many smiles, so much joyous fidgeting, muttering, and laughing in anticipation. I felt the bond felt between all of us, teachers and students alike, as a tether straight through my heart.

"This community has shown me true genius and I have finally experienced true love," I continued, "and, yes, it comes with challenges." I laughed a little, "I'm sure we all know about those."

The room chuckled and all the tension dissipated.

"So thank you for supporting us and we hope you enjoyed the show. Now here's one last song from all of us!"

I made eye contact with my guitar student, and smiled as he picked up on my non-verbal cue. He looked to his band's drummer and started counting "one... two... one, two, three, four!"

That night was the last cherished memory of our music non-profit before things took a darker turn.

Less than six months later, both Laine and I felt forced out of the space we had created.

We still feel the void it's left today.

6. Coming Out (Again)...

"It sounds like it's a positive result," she said as she gazed across the ocean with her feet off the towel, covering and uncovering them with a thin layer of sand.

Feeling the steady, reliable solidness of support I felt a surge of affection for her, my longest and in some ways deepest relationship. We got our jump start from my first edible experience with firecrackers on a Halloween-themed night over 14 years prior. I trust her with everything.

"I mean, unexpected results are usually the most interesting." She continued as she turned her sunflower eyes on mine, softer after all these years, but still piercing. The intensity of people's eyes had waned to an all-time low, but the pain seemed to be linked to overall stress, inflammation, and escalation levels (this has become one of the easiest "tells" I've learned to be able to identify as times when I should use more THC cannabis, schedule time under the weighted blanket, and be extra clean with my diet).

"Yeah, it's definitely interesting..." I trailed off, feeling apprehensive. The day before I had performed my first proof-of-concept experiment for my new cannabis research startup. I had expected to find one cannabinoid in the results - I had put in one single cannabinoid, CBD isolate, verified ~99% pure by both the third party certificate of analysis and our own in-house NMR, or nuclear magnetic resonance (the same technology as an MRI machine at the hospital, but at the atomic scale). The isolate was pure.

But the experiment didn't return the data I expected.

them through the mass spec, nerdy slang for a liquid chromatography mass spectrometer (a machine used to determine how much the molecules weigh) was even more surprising.

from my work during my thesis with synthetic cannabinoids. It had turned everything I had been thinking about cannabis and complex formulations on its head. It meant I had been thinking about my own consumption all these years without a major piece of the puzzle.

Over 4 years later, my personal experiment to optimize my cannabis use was still collecting new data and still evolving. A friend and colleague in the cannabis industry who was doing research on horticulture, or the art and science of growing, had recently sent me a new type of hemp that was high in cannabigerol or CBG. The effects were distinctive and somewhere between CBD and THC.

When I mixed all three types of flower together, high CBD hemp, high CBG hemp, and high THC cannabis, I found more reproducible, mellow effects. But this new proof of concept experiment showed me it was so much more than just the main cannabinoids in the flower. When smoking, dabbing, or vaping, the molecules in the flower are just the starting material.

"I think I am feeling..." I paused and racked my brain, racing through the analysis of my body sensations and finding the name to my emotion through the process of elimination, "...overwhelmed. Or I guess I'm overwhelmed at how I didn't see it before," I continued, "It's also like I could spend the rest of my life researching just this phenomenon and never make a dent."

I had entered an entirely new world shifting into the private sector as a co-founder, owner, and Chief Scientific Officer of my own project researching cannabis and its secondary metabolites, or molecules that do not contribute to growth or reproduction which include the cannabinoids like THC, CBD, CBG, terpenes that contribute to the aroma, and hundreds of other unique molecules.

I was always a believer in the entourage effect - or that the total effect of cannabis is caused by a combination of all the molecules, not just THC. But this was an entirely new entourage. This was a method-specific entourage and an environment-specific entourage. This was adding another huge set of variables upon an already impossible tangle of variables.

But within that variability was a possible explanation for why preferences for methods and strains of cannabis were so specific to individuals. And there was also the possibility for new optimal formulations and methods for neurodivergent cannabis users who were more sensitive to variations.

She laughed, "Researching cannabis for the rest of your life... Isn't that your entire life goal anyways? You've always had a pretty narrow scientific obsession." I could tell by her intonation that she was teasing me - a type of social interaction that I learned to understand, appreciate, and navigate with humor while high that had translated over to my sober state. Or perhaps it was that after all this time, my sober state just became more like my high state - calmer, less overstimulated, and with improved social relatability.

"Um, excuse me, it's actually called my special interest," I smiled, standing and feeling the sun on the tops of my shoulders. A rush of memories flooded my brain, all the years of shame and fear and hiding my obsession finally falling into place. "Could you imagine how different it would be if society saw it that way, instead of just labeling everyone a stupid stoner or an addict?"

"I don't think anyone wants to spend even a fraction of their time thinking about changing society compared to you, so most people are just thinking what everyone else thinks or what they're told to think," she stated resolutely. From the very beginning it seems I've gravitated towards a neurotype that doesn't soften the cutting edges of reality. It's probably necessary since I'm prone to living in a theoretical dream state.

"I wonder if it's possible to change what everyone thinks, like, so what if I call myself a stoner?" Even as I posed the question, I was full to the brim with doubt. Paradigm shifts, or significant changes in the overall big picture of a concept, were rare for a reason. Huge bodies of evidence build up to create several moments of discovery that sometimes take decades longer to be accepted by others, often well after a scientist or artist's death.

"Well whatever you end up calling yourself... I hope you know I'm really proud of you." She smiled while looking away before getting up and heading towards the water.

Suddenly my whole body and brain felt the solid, bracing feeling of acceptance while simultaneously the tingling tendrils of hope spun themselves up from my toes. My skin soaked in the energy from the sun, and for one of the first times in my life, I felt proud of myself, too.

We walked into the ocean together, letting the cold water wash over us. As my feet lifted and I floated over the incoming waves, I felt a specific type of calm carelessness come over me, a temporary stillness of my mind that was always followed by a whirlwind.

I am a stoner. I've known this as a fact, at the very core of my ability to be hopeful about my future existence since I was a teenager, blasting the Kottonmouth Kings "Rest of My Life" on my way to school. It was the first group of people I ever identified with and felt a connection to. It is still where I find my people. Those of us who partake often and regularly know this connection between us.

But coming out as a stoner professionally was something I struggled with, because my value as a scientist has been linked to my profitability, which for all of us in capitalist countries is linked to our productivity. Identifying myself as a stoner flags me as less productive, dumber, and slower than other scientists. Since creativity, passion, community, and personal health and wellness aren't viewed as positives in the capitalist system, coming out as a stoner undeniably reduces my overall profitability.

It was only from the privilege of stability in other areas of my life that I was able to even think about reducing that value by being more authentic, to choose to be unapologetically myself and significantly limit my options for how I could keep a roof over my head and food on the table. But if I was any less privileged, I would have never become a scientist, and I would have never accepted cannabis as my medicine. If I was any less privileged, I would very likely be in jail, unhoused, institutionalized, or dead.

I believe the most likely outcome is that I'd be dead.

Which means the difference between life and death for me was the privilege of being able to mask myself to gain access to knowledge and how that knowledge led to my ability to live authentically with my medicine.

And as I worked within the cannabis industry, learning the context and capitalist framing of the accessible cannabis erupting all over the nation, I started to feel an urgent, pressing responsibility to share what I had learned. Because I was beginning to see a pattern in the monetization of health exploitation, regardless of the industry (food/agriculture, drugs/pharma, health insurance, etc). The competing interests of profits stemming from a degradation of human health has created a clusterfuck that is our global food and health system.

For cannabis, this has resulted in a shifting interest away from funding for medical and into the much larger adult use markets. There is nothing wrong with that inherently as long as it doesn't infringe or damage medical spaces, but the truth is that often it does. Often the presence of an adult use market will wipe out the medical focus and crowd out medical caregivers and legacy operators struggling to transition to constantly evolving policies who have a much more intimate relationship and deeper understanding of the medicine.

This generally encourages passive negligence in terms of patient/consumer education, because there is no financial incentive to provide the best medicine, especially in newer, immature markets. The responsibility of learning about the quality and versatility of cannabis as medicine is put on the shoulders of the individual consumers, many of whom don't have access to starting points or the knowledge of how to begin to explore the options in a systematic fashion.

Historically, the community has always provided this education on a person-to-person basis. I have been there for almost all of my friends' first times. And I was taught directly by my friends and mentors, passing knowledge freely and blunts always to the left.

It's cannabis culture that is always about healing, always about medicine, but was criminalized and persecuted and even now is struggling to survive being completely washed away.

It's cannabis culture that has protected the quality of the medicine.

It's cannabis culture that has prioritized the exploration of chemodiversity for therapeutic value.

I hope we don't destroy such a beautiful medicine and I hope we can preserve the culture, including the documentation and formal evaluation of traditional and legacy methodology and knowledge.

But it's going to take a lot of public pressure. It's going to take changing the education level of the entire market and erasing years of prohibition propaganda (while facing censorship and other systemic barriers to free speech and community organization). It was the vision of a more educated medical community, armed to the teeth with biochemical knowledge, demanding standards, access, expungement, and justice that blazed a path for me.

The possibility of a future where the quality of the medicine is the ultimate focus and the driving force was the health of our community was so near that I was already living in the transition. The promise of the strength that we would hold together pushed me out of the cannabis closet, which also meant coming out professionally as neurodivergent.

I always knew I would have to share my story to explain the foundation of my opinions on cannabis as medicine. I wanted to be conscious, intentional, and transparent about my bias. I wanted to be clear from the start with everyone who would want to learn from me. It was a terrifying reality, but one I somehow always knew I was navigating towards.

It was like I was standing on a dock during an oppressive heat wave, a clear and cold lake below me, and I knew I would jump in, my brain already had committed, but I was just waiting for my feet to make that step off of solid ground.

And from the moment I closed my eyes and took that plunge, I was overwhelmed by the response. The number of people whose experiences mirrored mine and the number of stoners who were on their own journeys of self-experimentation was inspiring, validating, and, honestly, shocking. I never anticipated having such a giant community; I never imagined having the opportunity to teach so many and to learn from so many.

Your stories have changed my life.

Connecting with thousands and thousands of other cannabis users by sharing educational resources online has pulled the curtains fully back on my understanding of the stoner community. Countless stories of redemption, healing, acceptance, struggle, despair, and rebellion moved me to reconsider everything I had previously assumed. There is a significant population of neurodivergent people who benefit from regular, often heavy, consistent cannabis use.

We exist.

We are often discredited and labeled as problematic populations, forced to hide the mental health aspects of our cannabis use.

So we are often invisible, but we do exist, in droves.

I've found that a very significant number of stoners have been self-medicating, many paying the life-altering price of being treated as a criminal for it. And the lack of understanding and acceptance of cannabis as a potential therapeutic aid has contributed to the increased risk for our population through alienation and stigmatization. It's kept us a secret subset of stoners and has prevented the growth of community support that would focus on our sensitivities, our vulnerabilities, and **our unique therapeutic benefits**.

A case in point is the therapeutic value of the wake n' bake. Many systems cycle throughout the day, and the endocannabinoid system has its own rhythm. Lowest in the witching hour before dawn and at its peak in the early afternoon. Toking up first thing in the morning can have increased benefits that can last throughout the entire day and build a routine of consistency that has longer term benefits.

My morning medicine is a hippie speedball (coffee and cannabis), every morning. The mild stimulant effect of caffeine shapes the effect of cannabis for the start of my day. Way back when pharmaceutical companies created cannabis products, they listed coffee as the antidote to cannabis in their official pharmacopeias, because it can help reduce the sedating effects. But caffeine actually compliments some of the more stimulating effects of cannabis, which means combining coffee and cannabis can be a uniquely synergistic experience.

I have paired this with either a light workout, journaling, or playing guitar and have received unquantifiable benefits from starting my day with this combination of experiences.

It has been liberating finally being able to introduce research topics that stemmed from my community. But the benefits of coming out as a stoner reached even further beyond day to day quality of life and into the trajectory of my entire research career. It was this final leap to freedom that pulled me away from the shackles of my own pharmaceutical (academic) indoctrination.

And most importantly, this choice created an openness in my relationships with other cannabis advocates that has expanded the power of our collaboration.

"Do you remember the first time I told you that I was neurodivergent?" I asked my interviewer, looking off into the farm's greenhouse without feeling any obligation to meet her eyes.

She was also a PhD pharmaceutical scientist, a stoner, an advocate, and a close friend and confidant. She was the first person who I met fully as myself - a queer, neurodivergent, stoner scientist. She never got my pronouns wrong from the get go and it was a relationship built on mutual respect at a level I had never experienced before, probably because I had never respected (or understood) myself enough to show my cards so early.

Her area of expertise was studying the chemistry of the thousands of molecules from different natural medicines as early design leads for drug discovery. Our PhDs were kind of like two complimentary puzzle pieces and we fit together that way on a personal level as well.

We met through social media, because we were both creating short-form cannabis education videos and our followers kept tagging us together. I watched a video of her introducing G-protein coupled receptors, or GPCRs, as the main type of receptors that drugs target in the brain, including the CB1 and CB2 receptors of the endocannabinoid system. It was engaging, exciting, put into the context of cannabis, and she had reached millions and millions of people in less than a month.

I learned that she was also living in New England, only an hour away, and I reached out. We met up a couple weeks later and talked for hours over avocado toast about our lives, the biases and barriers of higher science, and the future direction of natural medicines research.

The hand of the universe felt heavy upon that beginning.

"Maybe?" she replied, "was it when we met up at a random park by a freeway to find out what percentage of people can't feel edibles? I think you had your puzzle cube with you."

Through community engagement, we had learned of an interesting and under-prioritized cannabis phenomenon. A lot of people can't feel edibles, even at very high doses (the typical dose suggestion for edibles is 5mg, but some had tried over 500mg with no effect). And this included people who had tried edibles from regulated and tested sources. It's pretty common for homemade edibles to be underdosed due to issues with decarboxylation or "decarbing."

The cannabis plant makes an acid form of THC (THCA) that is inactive until heat is applied. The heat causes a carbon dioxide molecule to detach to create the active THC. During the preparation of edibles, too little heat leads to incomplete decarbing which means more THCA and less THC, while too much heat leads to the evaporation of the THC produced out of the edible and into the oven or microwave space.

But many of the people who could not feel edibles had tried products from legal markets that were tested and there could be no question of proper decarbing methodology, which meant either potential issues with absorption or metabolism. It's known that there can be huge differences in both absorption and metabolism of drugs, but this specific cannabis phenomenon was unheard of to the scientific community.

This was just one example of how we felt community involvement could help prioritize the unmet research needs that could improve the medical value of cannabis. While both of us preferred smoking to edibles, it's undeniable that the controlled dosing, longer duration of action, and discrete (easy to hide) advantages of edibles make them an important medical option. And the first step to any research project is to prove that there is an issue worth investigating. Building "preliminary data" is an important part of fighting for the funding for research.

So we decided to meet up, film a short video, and run a poll that had thousands of responses in less than 24 hours, a big percentage of whom couldn't feel edibles.

To say it was refreshing to have found another scientific rebel who was unapologetically part of the cannabis community would be an understatement. After just a few weeks, we had outlined a collaborative new theory on the potential mechanistic advantages of natural medicines over single molecule pharmaceuticals... And planned an entire scientific revolution for the pharmaceutical field.

We had no shortage of ideas of how to chip away at the massive pharmaceutical barricades blocking research for preventative, naturalistic approaches. And we both immediately trusted each other in our intentions and authenticity in that mission.

"Yeah, that was it!" Despite all the hype around cannabis destroying memory, I still remembered the events of two years prior distinctively (perhaps because balancing THC levels with CBD may be protective for cognitive effects, or perhaps because the mystical memories always seem stickier). "I was in a cubing phase and I brought it with me, because, well, I was nervous to tell you about all of it; I thought you would think less of me."

That day was the first time I fully disclosed my diagnostic history to another scientist. It definitely helped that the discussion was over a joint and iced coffees.

"And when I told you that, you said, 'If anything, it makes me respect your opinion as a scientist more because you have lived the experience' and that really meant a lot to me..." I looked past our recording microphones and at the no-till field next to the greenhouse. A row of hemp cannabis plants lined the greenhouse, already over 6 feet tall in mid-June.

"Well, you've definitely taught me a lot about neurodivergence over the years," she laughed lightly, our eyes met briefly and I tolerated a no-stress, no-pain level zap, but then she looked away quickly with a knowing smile. She leaned into her microphone and moved onto the next bit, "and that's why it's awesome we can still create together. I think this is the first time we've even hung out since we both parted ways with the company."

That flawless summer day was a memorable reunion.

We had worked closely together for over two years as the only two scientists on an incredibly small team at my first cannabis research startup. It was an experience that I'm grateful for. It was critical to my growth as a scientist, a business-owner, and an advocate. But when I started to feel less and less connected to myself, less and less in control of myself, I knew I had to make changes.

It was a hard pill to swallow, but I had to accept the limitations and boundaries of my life.

I knew when I severed ties with my former company that it meant ending our friendship, and that we couldn't continue to work together on our personal theories and goals while she was still there. It was a stark change from speaking almost every day, tackling the same goals for over two years together. It was a difficult thing to give up and so I had held on until the last possible moment. I had made every effort I possibly could to have stayed, but I was losing, and I'm a very sore loser.

She had been my main support during that time, talking to me for hours every day about it, helping de-escalate me. This solidified her as more than a professional scientist collaborator in my life, but a safe space. It also meant that she had seen my brain at its lowest point in almost two decades, something that many relationships in my life fail to navigate through.

Seeing her again for the first time, I had wondered if anything would have changed. My brain can be a litter of red flags and she had seen pretty much all of them, first hand. I had prepared myself for the coldness, for the inevitable barrier.

I had prepared myself to see the fear that I've instilled in so many of those who've dared to get close to me.

But it never came. And I was confused by it, but it wasn't the first time she had confused me and definitely wouldn't be the last.

"It feels like a lot has happened since then," I said as I pulled at the jagged edges of a leaf on a nearby plant. "I feel like I'm both the same and completely different." I looked around at the back of the greenhouse, which we had cleared and raked just the week before.

My recovery had been turbulent at first, a total free fall that then gained direction through my grounding with the earth. I was lucky to have moved next door to new neighbors and friends who ran a small family farm. I asked them if they knew anyone who needed part-time snow shoveling help, and they said they always needed extra hands on the farm. I said sign me up.

Every week we hustled thousands of pounds of the best pickles on the North Shore. As the weeks went by, processing vegetables, hauling around compost, hand turning soil, and starting crops from seed, things just started falling into place.

Just as the first seedlings were ready for transplanting, I received a scholarship to a course on connecting the sacred, spiritual, medical, and scientific aspects of traditional methods of healing. The course focused on the classic serotonergic psychedelics and was built around indigenous wisdom as the central pillar to be integrated into modern medicine. While it brought up plenty of new questions and interests in the serotonergics, it also reignited my deep love for cannabis and planted the seed of a new personal project to focus on the spiritual aspects of my cannabis practice.

Laine and I took trips to visit and connect with our riends and family, I popped my first cannabis seeds, and settled into a gentler, more carefree sense of existence and purpose, something I had never felt before.

The interview came around just before the autoflowers were ready for harvest and we sat between two of my favorite plants, the aromas of the developing terpenes and flavorants wafting around us.

Autoflowering cannabis plants automatically start producing flowers after a short amount of time - usually only a few months. This differs from most cannabis plants which are photoperiod and start to produce flowers when the days get shorter and they are exposed to less light. The advantage of autoflowering plants was their speed, while the photoperiod plants have far longer to mature, meaning larger plants, bigger yields, and different aroma profiles.

Growing cannabis for the first time from seed to harvest, smoking the different timepoints of my first dry and cure run, experimenting with different forms of hash, and creating my own medicines felt like the clear start to the next chapter. It was blowing open a new and deeper understanding and respect for the plant that saved my life.

We sat under the shade between the cloth-potted autoflowers as the sun beamed down through the leaves above us. I was excited for what was coming next. I didn't know exactly where I would end up, but I knew the general direction I would head.

"I've been focusing a lot on the neurodivergent brain on drugs," I said.

I was going back to the very core of all my special interests, and looking at it from a new angle. It was kind of like starting over, but this time with a lot more experience, authenticity, and the strength of support from my community.

7. High Hopes...

We often only celebrate stories of recovery that look at the past as something that has been completely overcome, once and for all, the recovered hero completely changed for the better, never to be challenged again, but that will just never be my story.

The idea of recovery stems from neuronormativity, because it idolizes a specific brain state that is better and superior to others.

I am not proud of my past, but I am proud of who I am now, of the life I've built so far. I am honestly excited for the future, and it's taken a long time for me to feel that way. But I am just as disabled now as I was then, I just have more knowledge about myself and my medicine.

I know I would not be here if it wasn't for cannabis.

I am certain of it and that certainty has helped to bring me to another level of self-forgiveness. I used to be ashamed of it all - the severity of my brain, all the things that happened to me that contributed to it, and the path I stumbled along to get to the state it's in at the present. But I just didn't know any better and it's been a steep learning curve. I'm so far from perfect, I've made so many mistakes, and I want to prevent others from going through some of the challenges I had to navigate in the process.

Accepting my medicine was a big part of accepting myself, and fully understanding and embracing my use as medicine first and foremost had a significant impact on how I used cannabis. I wake up and smoke weed almost every single morning, I plan to do so for the rest of my life, and if I have a big presentation or some other professional obligation, I will absolutely still be taking that morning dose (if anything I will dose higher).

My typical routine is to dose low in the mornings (less than 250mg flower) with one cup of coffee, dose as needed throughout the day, and then higher in the evenings (on average about 750mg flower with an upper limit of about an eighth, or 3.6g of flower).

I'm a waker n' baker. It sets me up to be focused and have a great day mentally and physically. Later on in the day, the effects of my second dose are altered, more muted, because I already woke n' boke. It allows me to reach a better steady-state, or a relatively unchanging level of a drug in the body, which can typically be the desired end goal for drugs that work over long periods of time.

In a preliminary data analysis, my new research non-profit The Network of Applied Pharmacognosy has found that over 60% of regular cannabis consumers take their first dose before noon. So I'm not alone.

I also balance with minor cannabinoids, often mixing high CBG and high CBD hemp flower together with THC flower at a 40/40/20 CBG/CBD/THC ratio (See Appendix III - Other Selected Works for more info). I have found that this more balanced mixture makes the effects more predictable and reproducible, which important for me to be able to trust my medicine (especially if I have other obligations throughout the day). It also provides me with different options for different needs cases.

Using these ratios has kept my tolerance to THC fairly low. If I'm ever in a social setting where I feel it would be nice to feel "high school high," I can achieve it pretty easily - usually one or two hits of a concentrate or just a few hits of exclusively high THC flower. I actively monitor my tolerance and to make sure it stays at a low-moderate level - building in a consistent dosing schedule helped me find this beneficial range.

But I have found there are benefits for maintaining a certain amount of tolerance which is why I never take tolerance breaks. For me, keeping a decent level of tolerance helps decrease the anxiety side effects I can get from cannabis, regulate my sleep schedule, decrease my sensory hypersensitivity, and, most importantly, significantly lowers my baseline anxiety. I actually intentionally increase my tolerance to increase these effects if I need to, which is why I generally dose higher before any type of stressful socialization (conferences, networking events) and/or any activity that might involve motion sickness. (**Updated Findings in Appendix III - Other Selected Works)

While there are many ways that cannabis contributes to my health, if I had to list a primary pharmaceutical category for my cannabis use it would be as an anxiolytic, an antidepressant, and a preventative antipsychotic endocannabinoid system stabilizer.

But I am just one person and this is just what works for me. We all have our own endocannabinoid systems and we all have our own needs. Cannabis is a very versatile medicine which is both the best thing about it and a major challenge for its specific utility for people just getting introduced. Finding the best-case scenario for dose and dose schedule of medical cannabis for individual patients will always need to be tailored specifically to those individual patients.

I feel lucky to be able to contribute to a future where we have more guidelines to kick start that process.

There is a growing wealth of knowledge on cannabis as a medicine, both in the formal academic, medical communities and in the shared lived experience of medical patients. One of the undeniable benefits of the internet, social media, and the global scale and growth of communities is our ability to create and share information with lower barriers to entry. This has led to an explosion in the ability of otherwise isolated minority populations to find support and share resources and the medical cannabis community has been able to share experiences like never before.

We should increase our emphasis on the value of lived experience with cannabis, because as much as I love and value preclinical and clinical research... it's not reality.

Honing in on the real benefits and real challenges of medical cannabis use can guide and inform research, best practices, and policy. We are far from the optimal end-goal for medical cannabis in any location, but in many places around the world cannabis use is still illegal. This forces criminality on medical users, increases the likelihood that cannabis will be co-localized with other illicit substances that have an even greater risk profile, and creates a market for synthetic alternatives that are less regulated and have their own unknown risks to public health.

I am still experimenting and I plan to keep experimenting for the rest of my life, because we are always changing (especially those of us who cycle our hormones monthly). My story is not of one recovery, not of one singular journey to cure myself, but a story of constant, never-ending trial and error that has slowly led to a stable foundation of happiness over a very long, non-linear struggle.

And I know my battles are far from over because life is a constant transition and some of us struggle more than others with unexpected changes.

It's not so much that I've recovered, but instead that I've been uncovered.

And after shrugging off the weight of hiding my true self from the world, I lifted my head for the first time and saw an overwhelming surge of support from a caring and passionate community. The medical stoner community has been my community the whole time, but I am just now seeing us in a new light: we are nothing to be ashamed of.

We are not typical and it's more than just okay.

We are divergent and it's beautiful.

We often have complex, overlapping issues. We often have gastrointestinal distress that pairs with chronic pain and mental health challenges. We often have trauma. We often have a history of substance use. We often struggle to find support in modern medical systems. We often heal through community and have found each other through our shared experiences with cannabis.

Cannabis increases our quality of life.

Cannabis helps us integrate into society.

And cannabis keeps us hopeful and balanced, which keeps us alive.

The medical stoner community is significantly made up of a specific subset of neurodivergent people who are better at masking due to self-medication. This puts many of us right on the border of struggling to live independently versus being able to qualify for systemic support. This makes our relationship with cannabis a necessary accommodation.

For some neurodivergent brains cannabis can be **absolutely essential** for life, liberty, and the pursuit of happiness. The intimacy (dare I say devout commitment?) of this relationship creates a strong bond that is shared across different cultures, religions, generations, ages, and political affiliations.

Because all stoners have this one thing in common: we love cannabis.

It's not an appreciation, or admiration. It's love. It's a two-way, reciprocal relationship with our living medicine that often spans a majority of our lives (I'm currently at 54% of my life and it'll only keep growing). The amount of knowledge and perspective that we accumulate from being a part of this community, from collecting and sharing the lived experiences of not just ourselves but our friends and our families... that mountain of personal context for cannabis cannot ever be replicated by coursework in a classroom setting.

Medical stoners learn about the power of combining neurodiversity and cannabis through personal, intimate connections with each other (often taking turns infodumping troves of detail on each other around the circle).

Our stories are all unique, and yet we can see ourselves mirrored in each other through our collective pain and suffering, our explosive joy and liberation, our mystical faith in the unknown. We share a strong sense of responsibility for the health of our community and the protection of our medicine. We are advocates and we have conflicting emotions about the emerging industries and the effect it has on us. We fight our best fight, but we face compounding, systemic barriers and the downstream effect is significant.

We, the people who utilize, understand, and deeply love the medicine most, are underrepresented in academic education and research institutions, all medical fields, the commercial industry (especially the higher up positions in large multi-state corporations), and political regulatory bodies.

We are disenfranchised by our cannabis use, our bias, our radical opinions, our personal histories, our behaviors, our physical appearances, our differences, our identities.

We are often struggling to find a way to exist outside of the system, because we cannot conform.

We are shamed into hiding and our voices are devalued, because we are "part of the problem" population.

But we are the heart and soul of cannabis community, we've been here the whole time, and we are not leaving.

Despite our wealth of lived experience, we are not trustable, professional sources of information. We are up against a double weaponization of scientific bias that purposefully misinterprets the validity of both cannabis and the subjective internal experience of neurodivergent brains. And many of us face other societal prejudices that get slammed on top like race, biological sex, gender identity, and socioeconomic status.

I hope we can start to change that.

I hope we can start valuing the neurodivergent cannabis community, and by extension the stoner medical community, because accommodating us (by the principles of universal design) will lead to benefits for **everyone**.

Understanding the effects of cannabis on people who are hypersensitive (feel a lot with a little) and hyposensitive (feel a little with a lot) responders will give the best picture of the full spectrum of cannabis-related effects. Studying the average muddies the waters, because there is no average, especially for cannabis users. And many of us have our own complicated histories with pharmaceuticals or other drugs that create different medical benefits that don't exist for average populations.

There are no pharmaceutical alternatives that could provide the same nuanced, natural, and preventative therapeutic benefits with such low toxicity, nor will there ever be a complete synthetic replication. It's impossible when each plant has hundreds of unique molecules and can have millions upon millions of unique combinations of those molecules.

Cannabis is a gift; a living being that has been co-evolving with us since the beginning of life itself. We have shared the most sacred bond with cannabis, the bond of the earth, by directly cultivating it for medicinal purposes for thousands of years.

There are therapeutic and medicinal aspects to this relationship that are not quantifiable, they are ineffable, they are of a magical and mystical importance.

It's time for us to start investigating the benefits of that complex relationship in its proper context.

It's time for science to admit to its biases and limitations and be more cognizant of how it chooses to read between the statistical analysis. It's time for science to stop being complicit in the exploitation of human health for profit. And it's time for science to stop being silent supporters of the status quo.

Science was part of creating the stigma against cannabis and science should be part of making reparations.

I have high hopes that we're heading in the right direction, or at least that there's enough of us out there to make a real go at it all together.

The End...?

Appendix I - Key Terms

Here is a list of key terms used throughout the book that may need further explanation. They can also be used as search terms if you are interested in learning more about any of them.

---

ableism: a form of discrimination or prejudice that favors people who do not have a disability.

abstinence: the state of completely withholding from a specific behavior such as drinking, sexual intercourse, or other drug use.

ad libitum: Latin for "as much as pleases," a dose schedule of a drug that is as much and as often as the user wants.

alcohol: In chemistry, alcohol means there is a specific functional group on a molecule (a single oxygen with a single hydrogen, the hydroxyl -OH group). But drinking alcohol is a specific alcohol molecule called ethanol, and is a socially-accepted substance that produces intense, reproducible highs. Typically called a sedative, alcohol has other activities and the full molecular mechanism is still unknown.

alexithymia: the inability to easily name one's emotions or internal feelings

alprazolam (Xanax): a benzodiazepine, a common anti-anxiety prescription medication. Sometimes called xannies or Z-bars, they work by increasing GABA signaling

anandamide: one of the two main endocannabinoid signaling molecules that activate the CB1 receptor in a similar way to THC.

antidepressant: a category of psychopharmaceuticals that aim to decrease depressive symptoms

atom: an extremely small, basic chemical unit. Different types of atoms are called elements like sodium, potassium, nitrogen, carbon, oxygen, etc. These different types of atoms have different chemical properties which is the basis of chemistry. There are about 1.2 million million MILLION sodium and chlorine atoms in a single grain of salt.

autoflower: a type of cannabis plant that flowers after a short period of time regardless of the amount of sunlight

benzodiazepines: a class of molecules that are powerful anxiolytics (decrease anxiety) by increasing GABA signaling.

biochemistry: branch of science between biology and chemistry that investigates processes, molecular mechanisms, and substances (and the structure and functions) that occur within living organisms.

bipolar: categorization of brain functionality that is characterized by mood swings that have higher contrast and intensity than average.

blunt: a rolled smokable that is traditionally made by rolling cannabis in tobacco leaf (cigar wrappers), but more recently can be wrapped in thicker hemp blunt wrappers or other types of thicker, slower burning papers.

bong: a large water pipe that is used for smoking cannabis that cools and condenses the smoke.

bowl: slang for a small, handheld glass smoking piece; may also refer to the small glass piece of a bong set up that holds the cannabis. The shape of the glass is curved like a small bowl to hold the cannabis.

bud: slang for trimmed cannabis flower

Cali sober: a lifestyle choice where people abstain completely from alcohol, stimulants, opiates, and other drugs besides cannabis (and sometimes psychedelics)

cannabidiol (CBD): a common cannabinoid present in larger quantities in the hemp variety of cannabis plants. Non-perspective altering (Between Shulgin Scale minus to +1), CBD has many potential therapeutic benefits including anti-inflammatory, anti-anxiety, antidepressant, antipsychotic, and more.

cannabigerol (CBG): a common cannabinoid present in early development of all cannabis plants, but only present in mature flower in high quantities in specific strains. Slightly perspective altering (Between Shulgin Scale +1 to +2), CBG has many potential therapeutic benefits including anti-inflammatory, neuroprotective, and antioxidant effects.

cannabis: short for *Cannabis sativa, Cannabis indica,* and *Cannabis ruderalis* - an annual flowering plant that has medicinal properties.

CB1 receptor: The earliest endocannabinoid receptor discovered in the 90's to be the primary cause of the effects of the active molecules in the cannabis plant. It is present all over the brain and body and it regulates key functions that are essential for life.

CB2 receptor: The second endocannabinoid receptor to be discovered that is typically associated with the immune system. The CB2 receptor helps to ensure the immune system is properly balanced and is involved in hyper-inflammatory responses.

chemistry: the study of the composition, structure, properties, and changes of the universe.

chronic: an issue that is ongoing or recurring in flares, typically the severity of the issue is linked to baseline levels of stress and internal inflammation

codeine: a prescription opioid medicine used for pain

cold turkey: to immediately stop a habit

concentrates: very strong forms of cannabis products that are created by semi-purifying the active molecules from the plant in various forms (ex. kief, hash, rosin, ethanol extract, etc). Concentrates can be used to create edibles or topicals or they can be used directly.

corner or cornering: when smoking, only light a small portion of the bowl from the corner so that there is unburned cannabis for the next hit.

crude: an extract of molecules from natural sources that has not been purified

D.A.R.E.: a propaganda education campaign preaching abstinence only with minimal practical and tangible information for harm reduction, an acronym for "Drug Abuse Resistance Education"

decarboxylation or decarbing: the process of removing a carbon dioxide molecule and activating the molecules present in cannabis, mainly CBD and THC. It occurs at temperatures above 100°C (212°F, the temperature of boiling water and also why double-broilers are good ways to decarb without losing material)

demisexual: a person who has limited sexual attraction unless a strong emotional connection has been established

depression: persistent and unescapable feelings of sadness, hopelessness, and a lack of interest in activities that can be debilitating

dogma: a set of beliefs that are unquestionably accepted as true within a community, often without evidence or critical evaluation

dose: the amount of a medicine or other active substance given at any single time.

dose schedule: planned dosings over a specific period of time aimed to be optimized for a desired effect

drug: a molecule that comes from outside the body that creates an effect when it is ingested or applied

drunk: a specific type of high created by ingesting massive amounts (relative to other drugs) of drinking alcohol, or ethanol.

edibles: cannabis products that are made to be ingested. The quintessential cannabis edible is an infused brownie, but more recently chocolate, gummies, and even hot sauces or ice cream can be infused. There are also culinary cannabis infusion events where meals are intentionally enhanced with edible products.

eicosanoid: signaling molecules that the human body creates that are downstream of the endocannabinoid system and they play a role in inflammation and immune system responses

endocannabinoid: signaling molecules that the human body creates that activate the cannabinoid receptors; anandamide and 2-arachidonoyl glycerol (2-AG) are the two primary endocannabinoids. They are essential to maintaining balance in the brain and body

endocannabinoid system: one of the most important signaling systems that helps maintain balance in the brain and body including metabolism, the immune system, and overall activity; most notably known as the system that is responsible for the primary effects of cannabis.

enzyme: a microscopic, but essential piece of all life that speeds up specific chemical reactions. Enzymes are responsible for the creation and the breakdown of molecules in the body. Inhibiting or blocking enzymes is one of the ways a drug can create an effect in the body (ibuprofen inhibits the COX-2 enzymes).

escapism: seeking distraction (or entertainment) as relief from stress or other negative obligations to excess.

escitalopram (lexapro): a prescription antidepressant that is classified as an SSRI (see selective serotonin reuptake inhibitor) that is also prescribed for anxiety and other off-label indications like obsessive compulsive behaviors.

firecrackers: a simple type of cannabis edible that is made by mixing cannabis flower with peanut butter spread on top of a graham cracker, then microwaved in short bursts to decarboxylate

flower: the female reproductive structure of a plant; for cannabis, the flower contains the active molecules like cannabinoids and terpenes

fluoxetine (Prozac): a prescribed medication that is classified as an SSRI (selective serotonin reuptake inhibitor) for depression and other off-label applications.

G-protein coupled receptor (GPCR): a type of receptor that is involved in setting off complex domino effects in response to different stimuli that activate them like neurotransmitters, hormones, and other signaling molecules; GPCRs are the most common pharmaceutical drug target.

grandiosity: an exaggerated sense of one's own importance, abilities, or achievements, often associated with other neurodivergent traits

hemp: a type of cannabis that has lower amounts of tetrahydrocannabinol (THC) and higher amounts of other cannabinoids, mainly cannabidiol (CBD) or cannabigerol (CBG)

high: an altered state of consciousness and processing that is typically associated with non-prescription drugs

hippie speedball: a slang term for the combination of cannabis and coffee

homosexual: being romantically or sexually attracted to the same biological sex

hypersensitivity: increased sensitivity with decreased stimulus. People who need to wear sunglasses all the time are often hypersensitive to light.

hyposensitivity: decreased sensitivity with increased stimulus. I personally have a hyposensitivity to heat which results in me burning myself often.

hypothermia: decrease in body temperature. Activation of the CB1 receptor causes induced hypothermia and is one of the main metrics used when evaluating novel cannabinoids.

ibuprofen (Advil): a nonsteroidal anti-inflammatory drug (NSAID) that is over the counter for pain and inflammation

inflammation: a basic immune system response to injury, infection, or irritation that can look like swelling, redness, pain, and heat in acute stages; inflammation can also be systemic and chemical

infodumping: to share a large amount of information in an enthusiastic or passionate manner, typically relating to a special interest and the neurodivergent community

inhibit: in relation to enzymes, to block or stop the chemical process that they facilitate

intoxicating: the ability to induce an altered state of consciousness, typically associated with the consumption of drugs

LGBTQ+: an acronym for Lesbian, Gay, Bisexual, Transgender, Queer/Questioning, and other identities that fall under the larger umbrella of sexual orientations and gender identities outside the norm.

liquid chromatography: a laboratory technique that is used to separate and analyze different molecules that are in a liquid mixture based on their chemical or physical properties.

magic bullet: a concept referring to one single drug that treats one single target in the body to cure or eradicate a disease condition.

mania: a state characterized by excessive excitement, energy, impulsivity, insomnia, and elevated mood

mass spectrometry: an analytical technique that is used to determine the size and structure of molecules by measuring the mass to charge ratio of the whole molecule and fragments of the molecule after it has been split apart at its weakest points

mechanism: a detailed explanation for how a process, reaction, or system works including the specific steps and interactions involved

medicine: substances or treatments used to prevent or alleviate medical conditions or diseases and promote health and wellness

meta-review: a review paper that analyzes and overviews existing reviews, providing a higher-level of analysis and research than specific reviews

molecule: the smallest chemical compound unit, a group of two or more atoms that are bonded together

mysticism: an experience of spiritual or divine significance that transcends reality often achieved through meditation, breathwork, and other altered states of consciousness

natural products: molecules that are created by natural sources like plants, fungi, or microorganisms that can be used for medicine, food, or other purposes

net benefit: the overall outcome of any situation after considering both the benefits and the consequences or costs

neurodivergent: people who have brain functionality and/or processing that is different from what is considered typical in society, including but not limited to autism and ADHD

neurodiversity: the concept that differences in brain functionality and processing are natural variations in the human brain

neuron: a brain cell that functions by communicating with other neurons in a network through chemical and electrical signals.

neuronormativity: the societal assumption that there is one superior way for a brain to function, that there is a "normal" and that it is superior to all neurodivergence.

neuropharmacology: the study of the effects of drugs on the brain

neurotransmitter: signaling molecules produced by the body that are used to activate and signal between neurons or from neurons to parts of the body

neurotype: a term used to describe an individual's neurological profile, including any differences in their cognitive and sensory processing.

nuclear magnetic resonance: a technique that is used to study the structure of molecules by analyzing the shifts in atomic properties in a magnetic field

nugs: slang for trimmed cannabis flower, usually after it's been dried and cured and is ready for smoking

obsessive compulsive: refers to obsessive, often repetitive and distressing thoughts and compulsive behaviors that temporarily alleviate a constant anxiety

opioids: a class of drugs that activate the opioid system in the brain; powerful painkillers like morphine, oxycodone, and heroin are opioids.

overstimulation: a condition of being oversaturated with sensory input or stimulation like loud noises, socialization, bright lights, etc. Overstimulation can result in pain, anxiety, and shut down.

panic attack: a rapid, intense episode of overwhelming fear that is often accompanied by physical experiences like rapid heartbeat, shortness of breath, and sweating

pansexual: a sexual orientation that has no preference for gender identity or biological sex

paradigm shift: a significant change in the foundational concepts or assumptions within a specific field of study that can result in a new perspective or approach

paranoia: an intense, often irrational fear or suspicion of others or a specific situation; it can be accompanied by the belief of persecution or that there are harmful intentions in the universe

patentability: the ability of an invention (or drug) to be granted a patent that will give a corporation the exclusive right to create that product for up to 20 years

pharmacology: the study of drugs in the body

photoperiod: the amount of light and darkness that an organism, usually a plant, is exposed to in one day (24 hours); in regards to cannabis, photoperiod determines when the most plants begin to flower when the light begins to shorten after the summer equinox

piece: slang for a small smoking device, usually a simple glass bowl.

poison: a drug that can cause negative health effects, including death.

postsynaptic: the neuron that is after the synapse and receives and responds to neurotransmitters released by the presynaptic cell

preliminary data: early initial data that is collected in research studies or experiments that is used to form a hypothesis that guides future research before more comprehensive data is collected

presynaptic: the neuron before the synapse that releases neurotransmitters that go on to activate the postsynaptic cell

proprioception: the sense that enables the brain to perceive the position and movement of their body without vision

psychedelics: a class of drugs, including LSD, psilocybin, and DMT that can induce altered states of consciousness, deep mystical experiences, hallucinations, and changes in perception, thought, and mood.

psychiatrist: a medical doctor who specializes in prescribing medications for neurodivergent traits

psychoactive: in reference to drugs, substances that have the ability to alter mental processes, mood, perception, or consciousness

psychologist: a professional with a doctorate in psychology who studied the behavior and mental processes and can provide therapy, counseling, and assessments

queer: an umbrella term used to describe individuals whose sexual orientation, gender identity, or expression is outside societal norms

receptor: a structure in living cells that can bind to specific molecules or stimuli and begin complex signaling cascades (like multiple chains of domino effects) that cause changes in the cell

recreational: activities that are for enjoyment, relaxation, leisure, or socialization

retrograde signaling: a signaling process where signals are sent in a backwards direction from the postsynaptic neuron to the presynaptic neuron; the endocannabinoid system functions through retrograde signaling

scripting: in the context of neurodiversity, refers to the repetition of phrases, sentences, or dialogues from media or previous conversations in an automated manner

secondary metabolite: a molecule produced by an organism like a plant or fungi that is not directly involved in growth, development, or reproduction; secondary metabolites often serve a defense mechanism purpose

sedative: a drug that has a calming or sleep-inducing effect; sedatives can be prescribed for anxiety or for sleep

self-medication: the practice of using a drug, often without medical supervision, to alleviate physical or emotional distress and improve quality of life

sensory diet: a plan or set of activities, like working out, designed to meet an individual's needs, often used in occupational therapy for individuals with sensory overload

sensory gating: the process by which the brain filters incoming sensory information that helps allow the brain to focus on the important and relevant information while suppressing irrelevant or distracting input

side effects: undesirable or unintended effects of a medication, drug, or treatment that occur in addition to desired effects

smoke session or sesh: slang for when anyone smokes cannabis, typically in a group setting

social narrative: a learning tool that can help a neurodivergent person to digest information by outlining scenarios in a third-person story format

special interest: in context of autism and neurodiversity, a passionate and intense focus on a specific subject, hobby, or area of interest

spliff: a cannabis joint that contains tobacco

steady state: the point in a dose schedule where the rate of drug intake equals the drug elimination, resulting in a relatively constant concentration of a drug in the body

steamroller: a type of smoking device, typically made out of glass, that consists of a long hollow tube with a small bowl on one end; to use a steamroller the user places their hand at the back of the tube to control air flow

stimming: slang for self-stimulatory behavior, repetitive movements or sounds that some neurodivergent individuals, most commonly associated with autism, use to self-sooth, regulate sensory input, and express emotions.

stimulant: a class of drugs that increases alertness, energy, and activity, including caffeine, amphetamines, and cocaine

stoner: a cannabis enthusiast

symptom: an observable sign or experience that relates to a medical condition or disease, often used to diagnose or assess the condition

synapse: the space between two brain cells

synchronicity: meaningful coincidences that seem to occur without direct causal connection that indicates spiritual or mystical significance

synergistic: the combined effects of two or more drugs that creates an exponentially greater effect than the sum of their individual parts

synthetics: in the context of drugs, they are molecules that are created in a laboratory and do not exist naturally; typically synthetics are stronger (more potent) and more selective to a single target than their natural alternatives. While this comes with advantages, it can also create different disadvantages.

terpene: a large class of aromatic molecules found in plants, including the cannabis plant, that create the aroma and contribute to the flavor and overall therapeutic effects. Examples of terpenes found in cannabis can be found in other plants include linalool (lavender), limonene (citrus), humulene (hops), pinene (pine trees), and more.

tetrahydrocannabinol (THC): the main active molecule found in cannabis that is responsible for its perception-altering effects through binding and partially activating the CB1 receptor

therapist: a trained professional who provides emotion or psychological support and counseling to a person navigating a difficult time

therapeutic: relating to the treatment or alleviation of an ailment or challenge to quality of life

therapeutic minimum: the smallest effective dose of a medicine that can achieve the desired effect, typically with the minimum possible side effects

Title IX: a federal law in the US that prohibits discrimination on the basis of sex in educational activities and addresses issues related to sexual harassment and assault on school campuses

titration or titrating: the process of adjusting the dose of a medicine gradually from the lowest, sub-perceptual dose to the desired therapeutic dose while minimizing the side effects

tolerance: the process where the brain and/or body becomes less responsive to the effects of a drug or medication after repeated use and requires larger doses to achieve the same effects

topical: a form of drug delivery that is absorbed on the skin, but does not pass through to the bloodstream; lotions and salves are examples of topicals

toxicology: the study of adverse effects of drugs, typically at higher doses, on living organisms

typical: an appearance or behavior set that is considered normal or characteristic of fitting in with a particular context or population

typical-passing: a person who is neurodivergent, but does not outwardly appear to have a disability

umbrella terms: identifying words that encompass large spectrums of people like neurodivergent (encompasses autism, ADHD, PTSD, mood disorders, TBI, etc) or queer (encompasses sexual orientation and gender-identity).

vape pens: portable smoking devices that use heated electrical coils to vaporize substances, often cannabis concentrates or nicotine juice

vestibular system: the sensory system in the body and brain responsible for balance, spatial orientation and head to body position movements

wake n' bake: a cannabis session that occurs within the first 3 hours of waking after the main section of sleep, typically in the morning

weed: slang for cannabis, usually in reference to the entire plant or dried flowers

zolpidem (Ambien): a prescription drug used to treat insomnia and promote sleep onset and sleep maintenance

Appendix II - Selected References

These references are just a starting point. If you're looking for more scientific references on a topic is to look through citations of other papers of interest. Also this is a relevant time to mention a hero of mine that everyone should know about, Alexandra Elbakyan.

Chapter 1 - It All Started in AP Bio

Bidwell, L. C., Ellingson, J. M., Karoly, H. C., YorkWilliams, S. L., Hitchcock, L. N., Tracy, B. L., Klawitter, J., Sempio, C., Bryan, A. D., & Hutchison, K. E. (2020). Association of Naturalistic Administration of Cannabis Flower and Concentrates With Intoxication and Impairment. JAMA psychiatry, 77(8), 787–796. https://doi.org/10.1001/jamapsychiatry.2020.0927

Ghaemi S. N. (2018). After the failure of DSM: clinical research on psychiatric diagnosis. World psychiatry : official journal of the World Psychiatric Association (WPA), 17(3), 301–302. https://doi.org/10.1002/wps.20563

Huestis M. A. (2007). Human cannabinoid pharmacokinetics. Chemistry & biodiversity, 4(8), 1770–1804. https://doi.org/10.1002/cbdv.200790152

Wei, D., Lee, D., Cox, C. D., Karsten, C. A., Peñagarikano, O., Geschwind, D. H., Gall, C. M., & Piomelli, D. (2015). Endocannabinoid signaling mediates oxytocin-driven social reward. Proceedings of the National Academy of Sciences of the United States of America, 112(45), 14084–14089. https://doi.org/10.1073/pnas.1509795112

Chapter 2 - Not of Sound Mind

Edinoff, A. N., Nix, C. A., Hollier, J., Sagrera, C. E., Delacroix, B. M., Abubakar, T., Cornett, E. M., Kaye, A. M., & Kaye, A. D. (2021). Benzodiazepines: Uses, Dangers, and Clinical Considerations. Neurology international, 13(4), 594–607. https://doi.org/10.3390/neurolint13040059

Sun, Y., Lin, C. C., Lu, C. J., Hsu, C. Y., & Kao, C. H. (2016). Association Between Zolpidem and Suicide: A Nationwide Population-Based Case-Control Study. Mayo Clinic proceedings, 91(3), 308–315. https://doi.org/10.1016/j.mayocp.2015.10.022

Terry, K. J., Smith, M. L., Schuth, K., Kelly, J. R., Vollman, B., & Massey, C. (2011). The causes and context of sexual abuse of minors by Catholic priests in the United States, 1950-2010. In United States Conference of Catholic Bishops, Washington, DC.

Whitaker, R. (2010). Anatomy of an epidemic: Magic bullets, psychiatric drugs, and the astonishing rise of mental illness in America. Crown Publishers/Random House.

Yamaguchi, Y., Kimoto, S., Nagahama, T., & Kishimoto, T. (2018). Dosage-related nature of escitalopram treatment-emergent mania/hypomania: a case series. Neuropsychiatric disease and treatment, 14, 2099–2104. https://doi.org/10.2147/NDT.S168078

Chapter 3 - Bitten By the Lab Bug

Earleywine, M., Ueno, L. F., Mian, M. N., & Altman, B. R. (2021). Cannabis-induced oceanic boundlessness. Journal of Psychopharmacology, 35(7):841-847. https://doi.org/10.1177/0269881121997099

Guedes, A. G., Morisseau, C., Sole, A., Soares, J. H., Ulu, A., Dong, H., & Hammock, B. D. (2013). Use of a soluble epoxide hydrolase inhibitor as an adjunctive analgesic in a horse with laminitis. Veterinary anaesthesia and analgesia, 40(4), 440–448. https://doi.org/10.1111/vaa.12030

Hillard C. J. (2018). Circulating Endocannabinoids: From Whence Do They Come and Where are They Going?. Neuropsychopharmacology : official publication of the American College of Neuropsychopharmacology, 43(1), 155–172. https://doi.org/10.1038/npp.2017.130

Moncrieff, J., Cooper, R. E., Stockmann, T., Amendola, S., Hengartner, M. P., & Horowitz, M. A. (2022). The serotonin theory of depression: a systematic umbrella review of the evidence. Molecular psychiatry, 10.1038/s41380-022-01661-0. Advance online publication. https://doi.org/10.1038/s41380-022-01661-0

Peters, K. Z., Cheer, J. F., & Tonini, R. (2021). Modulating the Neuromodulators: Dopamine, Serotonin, and the Endocannabinoid System. Trends in neurosciences, 44(6), 464–477. https://doi.org/10.1016/j.tins.2021.02.001

Chapter 4 - Dosing Like a Scientist

Bang, P., & Igelström, K. (2023). Modality-specific associations between sensory differences and autistic traits. Autism : the international journal of research and practice, 27(7), 2158–2172. https://doi.org/10.1177/13623613231154349

Graczyk, M., Lewandowska, A. A., & Dzierżanowski, T. (2021). The Therapeutic Potential of Cannabis in Counteracting Oxidative Stress and Inflammation. Molecules, 26(15), 4551. MDPI AG. Retrieved from http://dx.doi.org/10.3390/molecules26154551

Moore, C. F., Marusich, J., Haghdoost, M., Lefever, T. W., Bonn-Miller, M. O., & Weerts, E. M. (2023). Evaluation of the Modulatory Effects of Minor Cannabinoids and Terpenes on Delta-9-Tetrahydrocannabinol Discrimination in Rats. Cannabis and cannabinoid research, 8(S1), S42–S50. https://doi.org/10.1089/can.2023.0062

Morena, M., Santori, A., & Campolongo, P. (2022). Circadian regulation of memory under stress: Endocannabinoids matter. Neuroscience and biobehavioral reviews, 138, 104712. https://doi.org/10.1016/j.neubiorev.2022.104712

Navarrete, F., García-Gutiérrez, M. S., Gasparyan, A., Austrich-Olivares, A., & Manzanares, J. (2021). Role of Cannabidiol in the Therapeutic Intervention for Substance Use Disorders. Frontiers in pharmacology, 12, 626010. https://doi.org/10.3389/fphar.2021.626010

Chapter 5 - Falling From the Ivory Tower

Andersen, F., Anjum, R. L., & Rocca, E. (2019). Philosophical bias is the one bias that science cannot avoid. eLife, 8, e44929. https://doi.org/10.7554/eLife.44929

Esmonde, I., & Booker, A. N. (Eds.). (2016). Power and privilege in the learning sciences: Critical and sociocultural theories of learning. Taylor & Francis.

Every-Palmer, S., & Howick, J. (2014). How evidence-based medicine is failing due to biased trials and selective publication. Journal of evaluation in clinical practice, 20(6), 908-914.

Sacks, Oliver. Musicophilia: Tales of Music and the Brain. New York: Knopf, 2007.

Chapter 6 - Coming Out (Again)

Khademi, S., Hallinan, C. M., Conway, M., & Bonomo, Y. (2023). Using Social Media Data to Investigate Public Perceptions of Cannabis as a Medicine: Narrative Review. Journal of medical Internet research, 25, e36667. https://doi.org/10.2196/36667

Kurtz, L. E., Brand, M. H., & Lubell-Brand, J. D. (2023). Gene Dosage at the Autoflowering Locus Effects Flowering Timing and Plant Height in Triploid Cannabis. Journal of the American Society for Horticultural Science, 148(2), 83-88. Retrieved Sep 24, 2023, from https://doi.org/10.21273/JASHS05293-23

Miyabe Shields, C., Kirk, R.D. (2022). Pharmaceutical Applications of Hemp. In: Belwal, T., Belwal, N.C. (eds) Revolutionizing the Potential of Hemp and Its Products in Changing the Global Economy. Springer, Cham. https://doi.org/10.1007/978-3-031-05144-9_5

Morena, M., & Campolongo, P. (2014). The endocannabinoid system: an emotional buffer in the modulation of memory function. Neurobiology of learning and memory, 112, 30–43. https://doi.org/10.1016/j.nlm.2013.12.010

Chapter 7 - High Hopes

U.S. National Archives and Records Administration. (2023, September 24). Declaration of independence: A transcription. https://www.archives.gov/founding-docs/declaration-transcript

Appendix III - Other Selected Works

Updated Dosage Findings 4/2024:

My therapeutic minimum is much higher than I initially perceived.

The two things standing in my way were access to medicine (concentrates) and the stigma.

On October 13, 2023 Dr. Riley Kirk, PhD and myself founded The Network of Applied Pharmacognosy - a new paradigm in natural medicines research that contextualizes biochemical data with lived experience. That night I decided to embark on another long, intentional self-experiment. In Chapter 4 I describe my previous long experiment completely abstaining from Cannabis for almost a year. The information I gained from that experience is what directly lead to my most recent diagnoses.

But this time I would not be abstaining from Cannabis. Quite the opposite, in fact. Since our private New England Naturals Nature Room launch party, I have been using as much Cannabis as I want, a pharmaceutical dose schedule called *ad libitum*.

I'm about halfway through the planned duration of the experiment, but I am confident in one finding: I definitely benefit from high, consistent doses. But I have been underusing myself for years. The higher doses continue to balance me in an increased beneficial way so long as my working environment can accommodate my neurodivergent variations and dose schedule.

Specifically, the higher doses help in working environments that have high social demands or sensory overstimulation like networking events, speaking engagements, or conferences.

And while my overall consumption did increase by around 3-5 fold total within the first month, in general it has plateaued. This means that I am not continuing to use more and more, but have found a new steady-state. This is an important finding, because it indicates that with proper intention there isn't a high risk for me personally to continue to develop a greater and greater tolerance.

There are a few other early findings from the first half of the experiment worth mentioning:

- **I love dabs**! Previously, concentrates were too much for me, because I was actively trying to maintain the lowest possible tolerance. But after increasing my flower intake, dabbing has a very unique benefit of de-escalating me from both sensory, emotional, and intellectual overstimulation.

- **Access to medicine is key!** Previously I was not as well connected to the community and lacked the financial means to provide myself with the proper medicine. Meanwhile I have been saving my insurance company thousands and thousands of dollars each month replacing pharmaceuticals and reducing other hospital costs. This financial burden limits access to proper medicine and is a health equity issue.

- **Discriminatory practices are common!** I was not prepared for the consequences of "coming out" as a high-needs medical cannabis patient... But increasing my dose schedule has resulted in a lot of pushback. Out of all of my "coming outs" this one has had a profound impact on my career. Professional discrimination in Cannabis is expected, and it is a significant and limiting barrier to entry for high-needs medical cannabis patients.

Excerpt from www.projectchronic.com/protocols-guidelines

**ALL OF MY PROTOCOLS ENCOURAGE RESPONSIBLE USE ONLY **

Intentional use that maximizes the benefits while minimizing the negative effects or risks to the user and their community is responsible use. There are many, many factors that can go into what is and isn't "responsible," but I boil it down to three major factors:

1. Do not put yourself in danger
Do not take an unexpected dose without understanding what the potential effects may be. Do not ever experiment alone. Do not mix or combine unknown molecules together. Do not participate in an activity that should not be done while impaired (swimming, biking, climbing, etc). Be sure to check out local laws regarding the legality, regulation, or restriction of any specific molecule.

2. Do not put others in danger
Do not drive or operate heavy machinery. Do not experiment while caretaking for another.

3. Have an intention and a limit
The intention can be as simple as to relax and have a good time, but be cognizant of it. Why are you seeking to

alter your perspective? Go into it with a known maximum for that experience based on the intention.

I would never suggest that anyone try this without the consent and supervision of a medical professional (nurse, MD, DO, PsyD, etc) or therapist who can answer questions on a 1:1 basis. This giant gap in knowledge between scientists and public service workers who keep our society healthy and safe is a huge problem. And it's a problem we are far too delayed in addressing and why I'm so passionate about sharing my information with everyone, including doctors, therapists, and, yes, even the police and politicians if they are open to learning about how these medicines can be powerful tools to help reduce harm in the community.

Cannabis Stigma Leads To Isolation and Increased Risk of Harm In High-Needs Medical Patients

Published in the Effective Cannabis Newsletter, 12/11/2023

The first time I inhaled that sweet cheeba was the first time I felt like my life could possibly, just maybe, with a lot of effort (and with a lot of weed), be doable. The quieting of my mind, the warmth from laughing until I cried, and the way the In N' Out fries exploded in my cheeks left a lasting impression. But paired with that joyous experience was the gut-clenching panic and anxiety that I have always been somewhat prone to.

It wasn't until halfway through my PhD that I approached my medical Cannabis use like a scientist. Through intentional trial and error, my understanding of my own endocannabinoid system and my medicine has been exponentially evolving every year. Now over 7 years later, my baseline dosing routine looks absolutely nothing like the first 11 years of my medical Cannabis use.

Looking Back Upon Those Difficult Years Is Always Painful

The deepest stab comes from how preventable a lot of it might have been if the information that I now hold in my head had been common knowledge back then. And it's a twist of the knife to know that we still face many of the same barriers to education today. Prohibition has left the general public with minimal knowledge of the therapeutic validity or the best practices for medical Cannabis use.

Unfortunately, the situation is equally dismal in the healthcare system; most healthcare professionals have been exposed to only a tiny amount of information when it comes to Cannabis. Medical Cannabis still remains a niche specialty for a small sliver of medical professionals. They risk their professional careers and insurance to take a stand for their patients and respect their lived experiences. But the majority still holds a deep skepticism that creates boundaries and inequities in the healthcare experience of medical patients.

Any patient who has been diagnosed with a substance use disorder understands the true consequences of being identified as the source of the problem, a drug seeker, a complainer, a psychosomatic nutjob. On my last urgent care visit, the doctor searched my arms and behind my knees for track marks before offering me a prescription for an ulcer-inducing dosage of ibuprofen. I respectfully declined.

The alternative is to lie. But this is a no-win situation if our goal is to have a trusting relationship based on reciprocal respect for each other's opinions, which includes the lived experience of medical Cannabis users. It seems to be a trend that the higher the dose of

Cannabis needed for relief, the more stigma that is associated, and the less likely it is for the use to be viewed as medical. Additionally, smoking as a method of ingestion over any other method creates a compounding effect.

This discrimination against a large population of medical users leads to deep feelings of guilt and shame. This can result in abstaining from a dose schedule that could be beneficial overall, or in binge-like behaviors when the patient feels "allowed" to medicate. And potentially the most dangerous consequence is that it often results in an aversion to receiving any health care at all.

While Cannabis has become more accessible than ever before, we still face the wall of medical disapproval. The narrow window of extreme conditions that allow medical Cannabis use to be valid in the eyes of most medical professionals needs to be smashed open. We've been suffocating and we need a fresh perspective.

This New Perspective Must Start From The Seed of The System: Scientific Research

It is the fundamental role of science to explore and support advances in humanity for improved understanding of the universe. The bias that exists in current society has been crafted and supported by years of research that was interpreted within a framework that many stigmatized medicines will never fit into. And so we must create and share research opportunities outside of that framework.

Medical Cannabis use is valid. Daily, multiple-dose per day dosing schedules can still be medical and can still be valid. There are unique therapeutic benefits to Cannabis that have not yet been formally investigated, but that does not invalidate the relief experienced. It just means we have reached an edge and that we must investigate it further.

Reaching boundaries, pressing up against them, and testing their strength, is the first step in breaking them, and I am optimistic about our collective and building momentum towards the other side.

Cannabis reduces (and prevents) my self-injurious and sui-dal behaviors... there is clear scientific basis for these therapeutic effects

Instagram Post from "@miyabephd" 9/28/2023

This "awareness month" always makes me sad and this year I spent the whole month finishing the draft of my book on the past 18 years of my c*nn*b*s use (and my life) which honestly made me even sadder. We almost exclusively celebrate success stories of full recoveries and that's just not my reality. For most of us it's a long haul and a lot of work to change our lives to be in more light than darkness.

It's in these heavier times that I have to be extra conscious about my use patterns because I am more likely to slip up and either use way too much or not at all. My brain and body are best when I'm not on a dosing rollercoaster. I benefit most from staying at a steady state. And it's really important for me to stay consistent with my medicine.

Because while there are a bunch of ways it helps me, my primary use for this plant is as an anxiolytic, an antidepressant, and a preventative antipsychotic.

It's scary to so blatantly open this conversation because I know this goes against what a lot of medical professionals and scientists advise... but it's true for me (and I suspect many others since we are the people with a higher drive to seek mind alteration). My most harmful behaviors emerge from prolonged states of stress, overstimulation, and inflammation (resulting in alterations of the immune system, skin, GI, pain sensitivity, and more). C*nn*b*s has demonstrated efficacy in all of those realms with low toxicity and deserves to be a candidate medicine even for "riskier" cases like myself.

Mixing flower for mellow and reduced negative effects (40/40/20 CBG/CBD/THC)

Blog Post on "www.projectchronic.com" 2/1/2023

I first combined these three different types of cannabis flower (CBD medicinal-hemp, CBG medicinal-hemp, and high-THC medical are all subtypes of Cannabis sativa) together when friend and colleague Dr. Allison Justice, PhD sent me some of her new CBG hemp strains. I've experimented with a lot of different ratios, but this one seems to be the most repeatable experience regardless of the specific strains/batches of the flower.

This made all the difference in being able to trust the effects of my medicine, because I don't get any anxiety, body chills, tinnitus, heart palpitations, or joint pain. I've turned a lot of people onto this blend and I want to share how I measure it out. Here's a video of me rolling one:

I keep my largest grinder filled with 50/50 CBG and CBD hemp flower and usually measure it out by eye, but the small scale pictured on the left was $8 at a head shop.

This base 50/50 mixture can be used with different amounts of THC flower added in. A breakdown of the different breakdown of ratios/doses is at the bottom of this post.

My favorite is by adding in THC flower so that the ratio is 40/40/20, so it's 80% hemp flower mix and 20% THC flower. In joints it is 0.80g of the mix and 0.20g THC flower. I like to keep the THC flower separate, because I do still feel strain specificity at these levels and like the ability to choose on the fly.

My other favorite go-to mixture is 25/25/50 CBG/CBD/ THC flower! That one is a big heavier hitting and great for social events.

In that case the weights would be 0.50g of the hemp flower mix and 0.50g of THC flower.

If you're curious how often or how much I use this mixture, I usually stick to The Multi-Microdose Schedule.

Reclaiming my spirituality through psychedelic exploration

Blog post on "www.projectchronic.com" 1/30/2023

My Grandma Kinu called us "lazy Buddhists" – and compared to the stereotypical, minimalist, sober, quiet, Westernized image of a bald-headed Buddhist monk, we are indeed very laid back. She raised me on a random hodgepodge of Jodo Shinshu (Shin/Pure Land) Buddhism and Hawaiian polytheism/animism. Her wisdom was rattled off here and there on a situation-by-situation basis as the need arose.

The summers I spent with my Grandma Kinu in Hawaii, sleeping on the floor of her best friend's kitchen pantry, are the most formative memories I have with nature. They are the core of my belief in the living, spiritual presence of the earth. She stressed our relationship with the ocean, the ocean's relationship with the island, and the island's relationship with us as infinite, as deeper than can be described in words. She told me stories of the wrath of the island gods and taught me to honor and respect the earth as a living being, as the mother of all life.

Back in California we attended Gardena Buddhist Church which calls itself "a uniquely American Buddhism of Japanese origin" that has "blended American culture and customs into" traditionally Buddhist services. I learned of the golden chain of love, of accepting suffering through release, of harnessing self-reflection, of the power of listening to yourself and others. In this type of Buddhism, we do not try to achieve nirvana, our entire goal is to live with the most faith in the Amita Buddha's teachings to be reborn in the Pure Land. Interestingly now as an adult, it reminds me of many monotheistic religions like Christianity, Judaism, and Islam; the reward for faith and service is a divine afterlife...

I don't remember a lot from my childhood, but I know I struggled with understanding some pretty basic social constructs. Starting in middle school, I began calling myself an atheist, because I didn't understand what that meant. A friend's mom called me an atheist at a funeral for another friend's father, and it stuck.

"This must be so hard for you as an atheist," she said, "since you don't believe in God or Heaven." I was crying profusely – really ugly, sobbing crying – because my friend was sad and her father had been kind to me. I knew I didn't believe in her idea of God, so I accepted that she must know more than me. I must be an atheist.

It wasn't until high school that I learned the term agnostic, and since I definitely believed in a higher power, I accepted that new label. I had no idea that being Buddhist could even be a label that was used in place of "Christian," "atheist," or "agnostic" because it wasn't explained exactly to me that way. I have a more difficult time generalizing knowledge than most people would think. Not that it really matters, because I am not truly all Buddhist.

It took me until well into my mid-twenties during my PhD to reflect upon labeling my spirituality outside of "I don't know what I am, but I certainly have strong feelings about it." I began seeking out religious experiences like fasting for Ramadan, attending iftar, practicing lent, observing the differences in various Christian sub-types, learning about the Hindu Vedas, celebrating Rosh Hashanah, practicing Shabbat, and closing with Havdalah. Every one made me feel closer to my own answer and I felt the common thread of love and community twist its way into the center of my belief in the divine.

But I could not feel fully supported in any of these major religions, because I am outside their range of acceptable behavior – in lifestyle, sexuality, gender identity. I also have many tattoos and consider them a central piece of my identity and relationship to my body. Plus the strongest emotional bond to my spirituality is from the time I spent with my Grandma Kinu in Hawaii and about my relationship to nature. I believe everything on earth has a divine connection.

Through deep self-reflection with the assistance of psychedelics and cannabis, I've realized that I'm searching for community and belonging. And just as lysergic acid amide (LSA) and cannabis helped me accept my gender identity between binaries, psilocybe mushrooms and cannabis helped me connect to my spiritual identity between categories.

My spirituality is undefined, but not unimportant. And through the exploration of psychedelics and cannabis, I will continue to grow my community and find belonging.

All of my research has been about the scientific evaluation of the therapeutic effects for mental and physical health, which are very real and exist, but neglected to take into account the spiritual and emotional component of that same healing. Now I want to bring the context of pharmaceutical biochemistry into my relationship with these living, giving beings as sacred medicine

Appendix IV - To Be Continued?

"Miyabe, you gotta help me, I'm tripping." My TA's piercing blue eyes had warmed and softened ever since we had started smoking weed together almost every day at lunch.

"What about?" I asked, unsure how I would help.

"No, like I'm tripping on acid."

"LSD?"

"Yeah, so help me if I have to do something," he dropped into a whisper and hopped his stool to the right, replacing the space with another stool. Thanks to cannabis improving my contextual processing, I knew that he meant for me to move and sit on the stool next to him.

When I got up out of my desk and walked towards the stool, he smiled and I returned it. It felt incredible to understand what to do. It felt like the most important thing in the world and still does today.

"Okay sure," I said, and then when I couldn't help myself, "what's it like?"

"It's great."

We went on to have one of the very first "deep conversations" I had ever had with another person. It changed me to know I could exchange something so significant with another human. I have a quote from a poem he wrote on the topic tattooed on my back.

Hours and hours later, we were still exchanging messages on AIM.

"You should try acid sometime," he wrote.

"I definitely think I will."

Miyabe Shields, PhD is a queer,

neurodivergent, stoner scientist and an avid psychonaut who is passionate about researching, optimizing, and advocating for complex combinations of cannabis and other natural medicines for neurodivergent "weird brains." Born on Tongva land in California, they now live in the Northeast at the Massachusetts' "fishing place," Naumkeag (also known as Salem or Witch City). They are the co-founder of the **Network of Applied Pharmacognosy**, a non-profit dedicated to prioritizing the lived experience by integrating the community with scientific exploration of natural medicines and Project Chronic, a small, renegade, neurodivergent education community. While they love winter backpacking and hiking, Miyabe is happiest at home with a lit joint, their partner Laine, and one chonky orange brain cell named Kitty.

"Here is the test to find whether your mission on Earth is finished: if you're alive, it isn't."

Richard Bach

NETWORK OF APPLIED PHARMACOGNOSY

"It is the fundamental role of science to explore and support advances in humanity for improved understanding of the universe. The bias that exists in current society has been crafted and supported by years of research that was interpreted within a framework that many stigmatized medicines will never fit into. And so we must create and share research opportunities outside of that framework."

Kirk R, Miyabe Shields C, Dautrich T, and Provost K. Introducing "The Stoner Neurotype." Poster Presentation in Cambridge, MA 12/09/2023

More info: www.AppliedPharmacognosy.org

"What is being done is ground breaking."

- 2023 Research Participant

The mission of the Network of Applied Pharmacognosy is to bridge the gap between academic research, the evolving cannabis and psychedelic industries, and the community of patients and consumers who benefit from these medicines with an emphasis on real world data prioritizing lived experience.

More info: www.AppliedPharmacognosy.org

Made in the USA
Las Vegas, NV
01 May 2024